Author of Mia's Journey

Bad
Karma

by JOHN REBELL

A CRIME THRILLER

Bad Karma

By John Rebell

A Crime Thriller

This is a work of fiction. Any resemblance to characters, companies, or organizations is purely coincidental and a creation of the author's imagination.

ISBN-10: 0982418264
ISBN-978-0-9824182-6-0

To get free updates on this book as well as free chapters for this book as well as upcoming novels, please go to :

http://JohnRebell.com

You can contact the author from the website with any comments or criticisms and will receive a personal reply as long you're polite.

Other books by John Rebell:
Three Pagoda Pass
Mia's Journey
Bad Karma

Dedication

To Lennon. You've made me proud every day of your life. You have taught me so much. You make my life worthwhile.

Acknowledgements

Ed Jamison for allowing me to view his unpublished manuscript "*The Devil Prefers Livestock*" and providing me with inside info on the secret life of the Vietnamese mafia.

"John" at B&B Meats for sharing laughs, deep-fried rib-eye steaks, and the workings of commercial meat grinders.

Tram Nguyen (My wife) for allowing me to use her day spa "Perfect Nails" for the setting of a scene in this novel. (By the way, ladies, the nail salon segment was all fiction and exaggeration.)

Theodore Koukouvitis for his insightful thoughts and editorial comments when this manuscript was in pre-publication.

I'd also like to thank the many readers who took the time to post reviews, both positive and negative. The positive reviews spurred me on, the negative reviews I learned something from.

Bad Karma

A Crime Thriller

John Rebell

Author's Forward

This book is designed to be a stand alone novella. It does however refer to past events in other novels I've written. It's not necessary to read those other novels to fully enjoy this one.

For those interested, the full story and background of Flynn, James Cobalt, (Flynn's Ghost) Mia, and Mia Lynn can be found in *Mia's Journey.*

The genesis of Max Cobalt, Ning and Wee are found in *Three Pagoda Pass.*

For those purists who want to read the books in the correct order, that order would be

Three Pagoda Pass
Mia's Journey
Bad Karma

Bad Karma

Des Moines, Iowa, USA
Present Day

"We do not remember days; we remember moments."

Cesare Pavese

Chapter 1

Flynn's life, and career, went to shit four years ago-the exact moment James Cobalt got shot in the head.

Flynn remembered the day James Cobalt was killed like it was yesterday. It stayed in the Technicolor of vivid memory every day since.

Flynn, was an 18 year police veteran at the time. He was doing an off-the-book job for Jeffery Prescott that spun out of control.

It seemed perfectly reasonable when it started. Prescott needed help finding his wife, Mia, who had disappeared.

The fact that Jeffery Prescott was going to be the next mayor, and having a few favors to call in if needed, was always desirable.

Jeffery Prescott was a sadistic lawyer who was almost elected mayor because his father, also a sadist, owned everyone in the state.

Flynn had always known Prescott was a few batteries short of a working vibrator, but he hadn't known the future mayor was a full-scale sexual sadist.

Nor had he known that James Cobalt was a one-man Marine Assault Unit.

Outwitted and outmatched didn't begin to describe what happened next.

Mia Cobalt/Prescott.

Christ, what a mess…

Before he knew it, Flynn was pulled in deeper and deeper. He set up a job with an inner-city gang to have both Mia Prescott and James Cobalt kidnapped. Mia was to go back to her loving husband, and James Cobalt needed to answer a few questions before retiring permanently.

The gang bangers pulled it off, but five people ended up in a pauper's grave. A small inkling of dread started creeping into the pit of Flynn's stomach then. All hell broke loose when the home invasion was uncovered by the press and to cover his ass, Flynn had to get in even deeper.

The call came in from the Prescotts to find out Cobalt's identity, and after determining who he was, to make him disappear.

Then the whole thing started going off the rails.

The gang members took Cobalt to an abandoned meat packing plant south of the city. Flynn found Cobalt trussed up and hanging like a side of beef. Cobalt had been beaten with baseball bats and tortured by the home boys he sent to do the job. Flynn hated himself for what he was involved in, what he was about to do, and what he had become.

He was a rich boy's hired thug.

James Cobalt seemed to see it all. He looked into Flynn's soul and called it for what it was. He forced Flynn to see himself, his life, and what he was turning into. Cobalt hadn't said a word to the home boys the entire time they tortured him, but he started talking when he saw Flynn.

Flynn remembered the conversation word for word, like it was yesterday...

"Your name is Flynn, isn't it?" Cobalt said to the figure in black.

Flynn remained silent and sat down on a chair studying his victim.

"Yeah, I remember. We met when you pulled me over. You can hide your face Flynn, but you can't hide the eyes."

"What's your name?"

"You can call me Daddy, if you want."

"A mystery man, uh?"

"No. I know who I am. It's no mystery to me. Flynn, what happened to you? This isn't your style."

"How do you know what my style is?"

"Letting girls get ass raped and beaten for the pleasure of sick fucks like Prescott is your style, Flynn? Is it a regular part of your job arranging kidnappings with the home boys? And when things get boring, moonlight as a torturer, and dirty cop for that ass, Prescott? How long are you going

to carry that boy's dirty laundry? You know he's going to fuck you over in the end, Flynn. It's his nature.

"What about when you pulled me over, Flynn, remember? You could have rousted me. Busted me on some bogus, bullshit charge. Beat the shit out of me for resisting. Splayed me out in the middle of the street in handcuffs, maced me, tazed me. But you didn't. You didn't use low class cop tactics. Instead, you played it smart. Played the game the way it was supposed to be played. You played it with HONOR," Cobalt raised his voice on the last word. "So, I ask again, what the fuck happened to you?"

Flynn collapsed inward on himself sitting in the chair. Cobalt's words hit home. As a cop, he knew from countless interrogations, the truth, people didn't want to face, worked every time. Even on himself.

"Fuck you."

"You're a cop, Flynn. I bet at one time, a good one, an honorable one. Did you join the force to be some rich boy's dirt bag?"

"It's not like that."

"It's exactly like that, and you know it!"

"We came up together. You know how it is. He helped me in the early years, and we kept in touch. We traded favors back and forth, that sort of thing. This thing with you and Mia, it got out of hand..."

"This 'thing' with Mia and me? Are you kidding me? I helped her get away from a sexual sadist! So now, you're going to torture me to get some information for your boss, is that it?"

"That's pretty much it, yeah. So why don't you just tell me. Save yourself the pain, and me the trouble."

"You're leaving out the best part, Flynn. It also means you're going to have to kill me because I know who you are and who you really work for. That's why you're here isn't it? Now, it isn't trading favors back and forth. It's murder one. Are you telling me that sick suck-ass is worth your pride, your honor, your pension, your soul? You'll murder for a scum bag like him?"

"Like I said, it wasn't always like that. Shit happens. Life happens, and..."

"And pretty soon you can't stop the merry-go-round. Am I right, Officer Flynn?"

"Yeah, that's pretty much it. It sucks and I'm sorry. You probably don't deserve it."

Flynn stood up, hooked up the jumper cables to the battery and came over to Cobalt. Using a large sponge he soaked Cobalt's chest in cold wa-

ter. He dropped the sponge into the bucket and picked up the cables.

"What's your name?" Flynn said, advancing towards Cobalt.

"Hey Flynn? I think you told me the truth just now. I think it was the first time in a long time you'd been honest with yourself. I think it also felt good to tell the truth for a change. I think you are a man of honor. For that reason, I'm going to let you live."

After that it was a blur. Cobalt somehow was able to leap into the air, wrap a hemp rope around his neck and within seconds, Flynn knew he was going to die. Flynn vaguely remembered kicking Cobalt in the face as his vision darkened. Cobalt's face never lost the expression of infinite sadness watching his death.

Then, Flynn was at peace. He didn't feel any pain or fear. He looked calmly down at his body. Then the next PowerPoint slide of his dying life showed Cobalt trying to resuscitate him. Flynn didn't even want him too. What a waste of effort, he remembered thinking.

When Flynn came to, he really was in a slaughterhouse. Over a dozen gang-bangers lay dead, piled up in the doorway. Another was dead in the break-room and another in the hallway. Speechless girls with blood all over their faces pointed out the front door in mute shock and horror.

Flynn took stock of his situation then. His service weapon, utility belt, extra ammo, and a one hundred and fifty thousand dollar surveillance van disappeared, along with James Cobalt.

Flynn, after facing and experiencing his own death, was never the same.

So started the slow demise of Flynn's career.

It was an understatement to say everything went to hell after the slaughterhouse incident mess came to light…

Prescott's wife, Mia, decided she had taken her husband's abuse long enough and killed him. At roughly the same time, Flynn killed Prescott's father and officially blamed it on Cobalt. James Cobalt didn't mind because he took a full metal jacket in the forehead exonerating both Mia and Flynn, and no one ever found out.

Sure, Flynn kept his mouth shut about the corruption he witnessed and participated in, and he was rewarded with a Lieutenant's position and all the perks that came with it. In return, Flynn was expected to look the other way when certain things happened to certain people. Flynn had his twenty years in and could retire, with his pension secure. But looking the other way got harder and harder.

Flynn got sick of the police corruption in his city. After that, he became disgusted with the political elite who pulled the strings, and were the main cause of the corruption. When that became known, he was set up and disgraced by the political establishment as soon as they found out he couldn't be bought or handled anymore. Worse, in their eyes, Flynn could no longer be trusted to keep his mouth shut.

Flynn started drinking. Then drinking a lot. That's when the ghost of James Cobalt started talking to him.

Flynn's ghost just watched silently, and said nothing as the disappointing drama of his professional life played out. He didn't have to. The feeling of disappointment was almost palpable. Flynn's ghost expected better of him. Soon that same disappointment started seeping into Flynn himself.

Realizing he had a problem, Flynn even went so far as to sit down with the department shrink. They, of course, wanted to talk about the Jeffery Prescott affair and how that had 'affected' him. Minutes into the conversation he knew bringing up the fact that he was hearing the voices of dead people wasn't a ticket to advancing his career.

Soon after it was "suggested" by his superiors that perhaps it was time to retire.

When that didn't work, he was drummed out of the police force over a bogus bribe set up by Internal Affairs.

Flynn avoided a phony conviction and jail time but wasn't able to avoid them taking his pension. Twenty years down the drain.

But it didn't even end there.

Though James Cobalt had been dead all these years, Cobalt still talked to Flynn on a regular basis. Broke, disgraced and a drunk, it was James Cobalt that remained his only friend and who suggested Flynn should start his own business.

It wasn't that Flynn's ghost was reproachful, or in any way unpleasant. It was the deep disappointment Flynn felt, like he was letting a beloved teacher down, that disturbed him the most.

Flynn couldn't "see" his ghost. Cobalt never appeared in front of him. There were no ghostly apparitions. There was no woo-woo in the dark.

However, Flynn could hear him almost as if he was standing right next to him. His voice immediately conjured an image in his mind.

It wasn't the image of the last time he saw Cobalt with a hole neatly drilled between his wide-open eyes and his brains on the floor. The picture it created was anti-climatic. It was an image of a patient teacher, a well-meaning mentor.

The only person who understood what Flynn was going through was Mia Cobalt. Jeffery Prescott's ex-wife. She also heard and saw James regularly.

They kept in contact, and Flynn felt a deep-seated bond and obligation to both her, and her daughter, Mia Lynn. It was the least he could do for his ghost. Mia Cobalt had told Flynn to listen to the voice because it was his "small voice" and it would always steer him in the right direction.

For the first time, his ghost and, mentor looked on with pride as Flynn started listening to the voice instead of trying to shut it out.

Flynn could almost feel the smile. His ghost got positively chatty and started talking about his wife Mia, and his daughter Mia Lynn, who was somewhere in Asia, his pride in them both coming through in his 'voice'.

Flynn was a disgraced ex-cop, turned unlicensed private investigator, turned underground street lawyer.

He liked to tell people he "solved problems" for a living now.

And Flynn's ghost approved.

What Flynn didn't know was that four years later he would meet James Cobalt's son, Max, and the wild ride would begin again.

"I am not afraid of death; I just don't want
to be there when it happens."

Woody Allen

Chapter 2

The carjacker pulled out a gun, leveled it at Max Cobalt's head and
said, "Your money or your life."

Max Cobalt had been driving downtown on his way to a final
negotiation with lawyers on a company he was buying. So far, it was a
contentious takeover. The lawyers fought him tooth and nail over every
aspect of the deal. Cobalt was a big boy; he understood the lawyers
were only doing their job. Still, their insistent nit-picking over even the
smallest details was making Cobalt think perhaps either he should add
a "tax" for the extra work, or go down in his asking price.

This is what he was thinking about as he pulled up to a red light in
one of the seedier sections of downtown Des Moines. A young bum
ambled up wanting to wash his windows. Cobalt waved the bum away
in the universal gesture of 'not interested.'

The bum pretended not to notice and in less time than it took to
look over, the bum produced a slim jim and had the passenger-side
door open and was sitting in the seat next Cobalt with a gun out. The
carjacker was wearing a torn sweatshirt and filthy long overcoat.

In contrast, he had recently had a haircut, and smelled of Axe co-
logne.

What the fuck? Cobalt thought to himself.

"Just do as you're told, and you won't get hurt," said the carjacker.

"Okay, what do you want?"

The carjacker leveled the gun at Cobalt's head and said,

"Your money or your life."

Cobalt thought that was an odd thing to say. A bit too melodramatic for a carjacking. A little too "Reality TV," and well,…rehearsed. Which was why he looked down at the car jacker's shoes and noticed they were five hundred dollar Florsheim wing-tips. The pieces fell into place in his mind with an almost audible click.

Of all the bullshit, cheap, tricks… thought Cobalt.

Cobalt sighed. Being a corporate raider, had its downsides.

"I have a better deal for you," said Cobalt. The light changed and he stomped on the accelerator. "How about my money AND my life? Why have one when you can get both for the same price?"

The Porche accelerated smoothly and rapidly. Cobalt expertly rammed through the gears, swerving into traffic, and causing both occupants to sway in their seats. Horns started honking on both sides of them. A few drivers let off steam with an extended middle finger.

"What are you doing?"

"Giving you what you want," said Cobalt. "You may have a gun, but I also have a weapon. It's called a Porche 911."

Cobalt jammed the transmission into fifth gear and was easily topping eighty miles an hour down a busy city street at midday, blasting through red lights and swerving around cars at high speed. "If I'm going to die, then so are you. You shoot me and this car goes out of control. At this speed, you aren't walking away in one piece either. By the way, I'd put on my seat belt if I were you."

Cobalt noticed the 'Police Parade' in the rear-view mirror and smiled to himself. Red and blue lights were flashing behind the Porche now as the cops joined in the high speed pursuit. Cobalt was gratified to hear more high-pitched sirens as more police joined the chase.

Cobalt rounded a traffic circle, the car flying so fast it was almost lifting up on two wheels, and headed straight down Grand Ave towards downtown. The police were in full speed, hot pursuit.

"I'll fuckin' shoot, just give me your money and let me out. I'll fuckin' shoot. I swear I will."

"You can jump out now if you want. Of course, I'm doing eighty, so the first jolt when you hit the ground is going to hurt.."

"I'll shoot," the carjacker repeated, "I swear I will."

"Then go ahead," said Cobalt, as he rounded the last curve, pulled into the circular drive of the police station, and stood on the brakes. Rubber was smoking from his abused tires, as he came to an abrupt stop, almost ejecting the would-be carjacker through the windshield. A dozen cops had guns out, and pointed straight at them. Cobalt put his hands up.

"You'll even have an audience."

The purpose of the car jacking was to ruffle Cobalt's feathers before sitting down with the company's lawyers. They wanted to try to knock him off balance prior to the final negotiation. They figured it would be a harmless scare tactic. Cobalt would give up his wallet and his car, stranding him. Cobalt wouldn't be able to make the meeting by default, giving them a reason to up the final price. Everyone agreed; five million for their inconvenience was a fair price to pay.

Instead, one of their lawyers was charged with felony carjacking, assault with a deadly weapon and kidnapping.

The cops especially liked Cobalt's wise crack about "making the city safer by having one less lawyer on the streets." By then, the news crews had arrived, and the joke even played on the evening news. Calls flooded into the police station as well as the news room. It seemed the population of Des Moines whole-heartedly agreed with Cobalt's observation.

Cobalt did rack up a few speeding tickets, but even the cops thought what he did was pretty cool and let him off easy.

Needless to say, the negotiation went better than expected. Cobalt, even agreed not to pursue criminal charges against the company's lead attorney in exchange for dropping the selling price by twenty-five million USD.

"Friendship is mutual blackmail elevated to the level of love."

Robin Morgan

Chapter 3

"I'm being blackmailed!" Thurmond Thompson blurted out, almost bawling to Flynn, listening to another tale of illicit love gone wrong.

Thurmond Thompson had a tale of woe. All of Flynn's clients had tales of woe. Mostly caused by their own stupidity. However, Thurmond's tale of idiocy was so vast he almost needed a video or a movie trailer to accompany it.

Thurmond sat in Flynn's east side office on East Walnut St, across the Des Moines River. It used to be called the East-Side Ghetto when Flynn bought it back in the early 1990's. Now the developers called it the "East Village" after they tossed the homeless and gang bangers out, and brought the yuppies in, and Flynn had ended up in the tony part of town by luck.

"Well then," Flynn said calmly, "Let's start at the beginning."

Thurmond Thompson was fifty-five, balding, pot-bellied, married to a shrew, and had three ungrateful, spoiled kids. He was unhappy about most of his adult life. His family also owned the only bank and commercial real estate company in a small town in Western Iowa. He was cruising gay Internet chat rooms and struck up an unlikely friendship with "Aaron."

"Of course, I'm not gay you understand," he was quick to tell Flynn. "I just wanted a male friend away from my family."

"I understand completely," Flynn said, not understanding at all.

"Well, one thing led to another."

"Of course, it did. These things do. What happened?"

What happened was that "Aaron" was being locked up in a drug re-hab center by his rich father, which cost twenty thousand a month. The rehab center didn't want to release him because they were making big bucks so they kept on making up psychological problems. The father didn't want him to leave, because it was easier to pay 20K a month than it was to deal with a snotty adult baby.

So started the unlikely friendship, a twenty-five-year-old "boy" looking for a father, and a much older man looking for a son.

Thurmond was so taken with Aaron, they started communicating privately online, and soon Aaron had him convinced to ditch his wife, get divorced, and live the life he *deserved*.

Thurmond showed Flynn a picture of Aaron, smiling brightly, in a cap and gown on graduation day. He had a fresh, blond, clean cut, 'boy-next-door' look about him. Flynn was sure the photo was pulled off of Facebook, but he kept quiet.

In due time as Aaron ran the line ran out, our hero swallowed every hook, line, and kinky fetish that Aaron threw into the sexual waters like chum.

During those heady days, Thurmond also sent him money ($500) so that he could get those little "extras" needed in captivity. His evil father wouldn't pay for them, of course. He sent more money to pay for an "independent specialist" ($1000) to evaluate Aaron's condition. Which Aaron promptly reported "proved" that he was clean, problem free, and rehabilitated. Granted, Thurmond never saw the report, but the money and logistics were handled professionally by a firm in New York City that specialized in these kinds of things and he had no reason to doubt them.

Flynn resisted the urge to roll his eyes.

Then the big day came. Aaron was going to be released! Together, they had beaten the evil father and greedy rehab establishment! It was such a momentous occasion Aaron thought they should celebrate by going on a three-day gay cruise up the Mississippi River on a paddle wheel boat, no less.

Thurmond, unable to keep his lust bridled, couldn't agree more. Three days alone and sharing the same room, he knew his ship had come in, so to speak. He sprang for the 'Captain's Cabin' at another thousand dollars a day, for his chance at the life he deserved. He even filed divorce papers on the shrew wife and spoiled brats...

Let the Battle Ax chomp on that for a while.

All arrangements and money transfers were handled by the same New York firm. See…he had the receipts to prove it!

Once Aaron had gotten close to five thousand dollars out of him, his financials verified, and wrapped securely in a net of his own kinkiness, it was time for Aaron to reel the Big Kahuna in. That's when Thurmond, almost in tears, handed over the last email to Flynn.

"Dearest Thurmond," the email began.

"I know this may come as a shock, but you're an idiot. So much of an idiot I'm going to give you a choice. You can pay me $100,000 and our secret affair will remain secret. If not, then I'll be forced to mail all those smutty pictures of you and your penis to your wife, father, and your church. Along with your emails telling all the kinky things you'd like to do. Not to mention the town paper where you live and anyone else I can think of.

"So here's what you're going to do. You'll transfer the money via the company in New York you've grown so fond of. You have seven days. One week from today if I don't see that money, your wife, family, church, and everyone else in your town will know what you like to do in your spare time. I've attached a picture you sent me of yourself in girl's panties and bra to remind you of our good times together."

"And you got this yesterday?" Flynn asked.

"Yes. Is there anything you can do?"

Flynn spun in his chair and faced the computer. He punched Thurmond's 'secret' username into Gmail.

"What's your password?"

"Babyboy" Thurmond almost whispered.

This time Flynn did roll his eyes, but not before turning back to his computer and away from his client. Flynn typed in the password, pulling up his inbox. He located the email, copied the IP address it was sent from, then did a 'Whois' back-trace on the numbered account. It came back to a location in Des Moines.

Flynn knew most of the scammers in Des Moines and there was only one person who had the sophistication to pull off something of this scope.

"Yeah, I think I can help," Flynn said, deadpan.

"Everyone has favorite criminals. Mine are pimps. We can all rob a bank; we can all sell drugs. Being a pimp is a whole other thing."

Chris Rock

Chapter 4

"The trick with the hoes," Lamar said, stroking his goatee, "Is to make sure they knows they hoes. You feel me?"

Lamar was a pimp and lots of other things no one was quite sure of. He didn't dress 'pimp flashy', but he had a certain style even so. And Lamar's style was…different.

Lamar watched Flynn come up the alley as he 'schooled' the young gang bangers, sitting on an upturned five-gallon pail. They sat cross-legged before him in the dirty alley. A sort of modern day, inner-city Aristotle.

Lamar was a legend to these kids. He made more money than drug dealers, and everyone left him alone. Rumor had it, Lamar could get rough if the situation called for it. But it rarely did. Lamar liked to say, to paraphrase Teddy Roosevelt, he talked softly and carried a pump shotgun.

"Now every hoe has a hole in her heart. Once you figure out the hole, and start to fill that hole, them sorry bitches can't get enough! Them bitches be your hoe for life!"

Flynn eased up slowly on the group. He knew all of them made him for cop the minute he got out of his car. There was no use trying to fake the kids or Lamar. Lamar knew he was coming before probably even Flynn did.

"Now, I'm gonna school ya," continued Lamar, "Every hoe want one of two things: She be wantin' security if she be havin' an excitin' life, like your mommas, or she be wantin' excitmen' if she have a boring life, like a soccer mom out in the burbs. Ya feel?" Lamar looked over at Flynn and nodded. "Ask Flynn. Ain't that right, Flynn?"

"If you say so, Lamar."

"When do you get to slap de hoes around?" Asked a kid named Poot.

"You ain't been listenin'. You do it my way, you don't have to slap no bitches aroun'. Hoes with bruises don' make money. You do it my way, she be wantin' to please you. You hearin me?"

"My Pa, he slap em' around plenty. He say you have to."

"Well, then maybe you and your Pa need to go catch a felony assault, maybe then you be understandin'."

"When you were on the force, Flynn, what was the number-one reason for busting a pimp?"

"Agg. Assault. Beating the girls."

"Now you see," Lamar continued, "The thing about them hoe holes, is once you fill them, you can also drain them. You can push their buttons, you feel me? Now, if you be thinking some hoe be getting in your grill, you just push a button, and she be set back on her ass. You don't need to slap them hoes. But every now and again, you jus' push one of her buttons. Otherwise they be walking all over you. True that.

"That there, is Pimpology 101. Class dismissed. Get out of here."

In spite of his polished, home boy, ghetto twang, Flynn knew Lamar was no dummy. He was self-educated and held a number of college degrees. He never bothered to get a diploma though. He just kept going to school. He didn't want credits, or PHD after his name. He couldn't use them anyway in his line of work. Lamar just wanted to learn.

He was always trying to keep these kids in school and keep them learning. Which was more than the justice system, school system, social services, and their parents combined, tried to do.

"Pimpology 101?" Flynn shook his head in amusement once they were alone.

"Someone's got to show these kids something different than their ways. I don't see anyone else, do you?" all trace of the ghetto and 'ebonics' gone from Lamar's voice.

"No, I don't."

"So, to what do I owe the pleasure?"

"I might need you to back off one of your scams."

"Then I might need your help scaring the shit out of one of my competitors."

"Mine first," Flynn said. "You still owe me for getting that idiot DOP off your back years ago."

Lamar looked at Flynn thinking of how many years they went back, weighing the offer.

"I remember it differently. I didn't ask you to have 'Rambo' wipe out half the ghetto. That was your doing."

"Yeah, well, you benefited from it. It gave you new territory."

"I would have gotten it anyway. What do you need?"

"Tell me about your boy to men chat room scams."

Lamar burst out laughing. "B2M? Why? Getting a little lonely in the East Village, Flynn?"

Flynn smiled, taking the ribbing. "Don't make me show you my weapon, asshole."

"What do you want to know?"

"How does it work?"

"Well, one of my 'community outreach' programs is teaching the kids about the Internet. I get them to hang out in the gay chat rooms, where they troll for losers."

"Are you shitting me?"

"There are a lot of positive benefits," Lamar said, slightly offended.

"Like what?"

"They have to talk, read, and write, correct whitebread English, for one. That means they've got to study their little asses off to learn a different way of speaking. It teaches them how to research topics and people over the Internet. They never had a reason to learn how to read before. I gave them a reason."

"Which is?"

"They get 50% of the take. I got kids making thousands a week. It's better than the streets, guns and drugs."

He had a point.

"Okay, whatever. How does the scam work?"

Lamar looked at Flynn, sizing him up, "If you want to know how the scam works, then you have to see it in action."

"Lead the way," Flynn said.

"First, we need to take a ride," Lamar said.

Together both men walked down the garbage strewn alley back to the street. There were dumpsters lining each side of the alley behind restaurants, smelling of rotten food left in the sun. The asphalt was greasy and slippery with organic matter ground to a pulp under many feet. When they got to the street, Lamar indicated right by nodding his head towards his car. They stopped beside a silver Prius, and Lamar clicked it open with the remote.

"What kind of self-respecting pimp drives a Prius?" Flynn said in disbelief. "Shouldn't you have like a gold El Dorado or something?"

Flynn had to stand outside the car, bending down, working the seat levers backwards and down before he could even get in.

"The kind of self-respecting pimp who believes Global Warming is a problem. The kind that doesn't want to support oil wars in the Middle East, the kind that..."

"Okay, okay. Pimps around the country would be ashamed. I'm almost embarrassed to be seen with you. What's next for the enlightened pimp...saving the whales?"

Lamar took a right at a stop sign on MLK Boulevard, and headed south towards the light industrial section of the city.

"Yeah, you're a delicate little flower, Flynn." Lamar said, cruising over the Des Moines River Bridge.

"Flynn, I hate to break it to you, but we don't call ourselves 'pimps' anymore. That is very 1980. I'm a 'Human Resource Manager.'"

"Yeah, right. I'm also your aunt Mabel."

They pulled neatly into a parking lot with a cinder block low rise and very little else. There was a dirt parking lot, a few cars, and a sign that said "Allied Consultants, Inc." Lamar got out and was already striding for the door.

"You coming?"

"Only if I can get out of your go-kart. I might be trapped in here forever."

Lamar waited patiently for Flynn as he lifted himself out of the Prius like he was stuck in a sardine can.

When Flynn opened the door, the world changed.

Inside the shabby cinder block office it became a quiet hub of activity and focus. There were glass cubicles set along the wall in a 'U' shape around the entire building. Or at least, one side was glass so that it was open to the outside world. The other three walls were decorated differently, depending on what was needed for the scam.

Some were decorated as dorm rooms, some as girl's bedrooms, one as a hospital room, another as an office, etc.

About a dozen kids between the ages of fifteen and twenty worked quietly at laptops as they researched their marks while simultaneously talking to them via chat. If a mark insisted on video, they could turn it on and tease them. The background was congruent with whatever persona the kids chose to play. About half of them were gang bangers, the other half were college kids. Half were males, half females, white, black, and Hispanic. There were also enclosed rooms set aside, set up to look like college dorms or bedrooms if they needed to add a touch of realism and sex chat by video.

Flynn was struck speechless. This was a well-planned, well-organized, well-tuned blackmail racket. These weren't your normal, truant, joint smoking kids either. They all wore different clothes. Some looked like college kids in sweats and sneakers. Others wore suits. One kid was dressed like a football star, another one of the girls was a varsity cheerleader, and another, a soccer mom.

"The trick here is these kids have to become who they are portraying, " Lamar said, putting on a telephone head set. "This means research and study. They learn not only to write and act like the kids they portray, but also psychology, sociology, selling, persuasion, NLP, and about a dozen other things I can't think of. These kids are brilliant. Every single one of these kids are from the ghetto. See those college kids over there? Not a single one of them made it past sixth grade, let alone high school. They were abandoned by their parents to fend for themselves."

"Now they speak, read, write, and act the parts they play. Not only that, but these kids play multiple parts. Today that one is a cheerleader, tomorrow she'll be a homeless runaway, the day after a…"

"I get the picture," Flynn said, awed.

"So what do you want to know?"

"You got a kid named Aaron running a scam on a banker in Western Iowa?"

"Anyone here named Aaron running a B2M scam?" Lamar spoke quietly into the headset attached to his ear.

"I am," said a boy, coming out of a glass cubicle, no more than sixteen and dressed in gang colors. He had an afro and an intricate tribal tattoo running up his neck to his lower jaw.

Not the Aaron in Thurmond's picture, that's for sure, thought Flynn.

"Run it down for me," Lamar said to the boy.

"Rehab scam. Been jerking his chain for about three months. We reeled him in this week. It's a hundred thousand dollar payday," the boy said, summarizing it up like a pro. He could have been talking about stocks. Not a trace of the streets in his voice. "He thinks I'm a blond, white boy in rehab with a mean father who won't let him leave. He's a rich, closet queen and I nailed him. I even got him to file divorce on his wife to be with me."

"I need you to back off of him," Flynn said, directly to the boy.

"Fuck you, Grandpa. I'm about to collect. Lamar, who is this, Whitebread?"

"I'm asking myself that question, too," Lamar said, looking at Flynn. "Why should we?"

"Because I'm asking politely?"

"So let me get this straight. I lose fifty large, Aaron here loses fifty grand, and in return, you'll be *polite* to us?"

"Well, when you put it that way, I guess I am a little on the light side of this deal. How about if I owe you one instead, and I won't be polite?"

"Didn't you hear, Flynn? The Po-Po tossed your raggedy ass out. You ain't got suction downtown no more with the boys in blue." The street was creeping back into Lamar's voice. "I got a better idea. I need a little help with a problem of mine. You solve my problem, maybe we can solve yours."

"I need you to solve my problem fast."

"Then you need to solve mine even quicker."

"Wait a minute, Lamar," said Aaron, "I've been working this guy three months. What do I get?"

"I'll take care of you, shorty. You have my word. What about it, Flynn?"

"What do you need?"

"The Vietnamese mafia wants to push me out of pimping. I need to push back. At the very least, I want the long, black cloud of bad Karma to visit them."

"What do you got in mind?"

"I need you to do what you do best, run surveillance and setup. One thing you need to know. These fuckers play for keeps," Lamar said.

"What is said in the nail salon, stays in the nail salon."

Sign in Las Vegas nail salon

Chapter 5

"This woman's got the biggest tits I've ever seen!"

Tram Ngoc, a Vietnamese nail technician, said to the woman she was working with in Vietnamese.

Assured she wasn't being understood by her customer, the nail tech continued.

"Her ass is so big I wonder why she doesn't fall over," the nail tech smiled up at her customer.

"If she did, she would just bounce back," another nail said tech from across the room in the same language.

"What did she say?" Asked the customer under discussion.

"I say you have nice hair, she agree with me," the nail tech said, lying smoothly.

"Oh, thank you," the customer primped her hair with the compliment, not understanding the conversation at all.

"What happened to her hair? Did she stick a finger in a light socket?" chimed in another from across the room.

"Her mommas are so big, I could use them as pontoons to cross the Mekong River!" Another nail tech said.

"Why do American women all have such big bongos and fat asses?"

"What are they talking about now?" Asked the customer.

"Everyone say they like your shoes," Tram replied.

"Oh, well, thank you."

"They have fat asses because they sit on them all day long," the nail tech sang out to the group. *"Their American husbands even let them!"*

This got a chorus of agreement from the girls at the nail salon.

Ning listened to the conversation. She couldn't speak Vietnamese, but her mother tongue, Thai, belonged to the same family of languages and she could understand it well enough.

The Vietnamese nail tech glanced at her, wondering if she understood their language.

"Where you from?"

"China," Ning said, lying as well.

"So you understand what we say?"

Ning decided to play dumb.

"No, I can only speak Cantonese."

Ning watched the girls around her. She could tell most of them were uneducated and unlicensed. A few, she knew from their complexion and dental work, came from what used to be North Vietnam. Most of the techs paid no attention whatsoever to what they were doing. They just chatted in Vietnamese to each other over the customer's head, but rarely to the customer. Looking around, Ning noticed many were using unsanitary practices and dirty instruments. They weren't sanitizing the instruments between customers. She made a mental note not to come to this salon again.

Ning also understood most of them bought their licenses in diploma mills. They would travel to Florida or California and buy a bogus license, then bring it back to the state where they lived. The state, having reciprocal licensing agreements, would then give them a license to work in the home state. In this way, the Vietnamese got around the licensing laws. This allowed them to spread all over the country and effectively take over the nail industry in just about every state and town. She noticed most of the women were young. There were a few very young ones. Teenagers who should be in school. Strange.

"How did you get your job?" Ning asked her nail tech.

"My uncle asked me to come work for him," the nail tech said evasively, shutting down the conversation. Ning knew, the American translation and meaning for 'uncle' meant a blood relative. The Asian translation was used for just about any older male. Vietnamese always spoke in terms of family, but it had more to do with age. 'Grandfather' was man about the age of their grandfather. 'Uncle' was a man about the age of their father's brother. 'Uncle' could also mean mentor. Blood relation had little to do with it. It was like certain races saying 'brother' meaning any male or friend.

"Have you been in the US long?"

Ning noticed nervous glances from the other nail techs now.

"Yes, many year."

"My God, this woman's feet stink!" Said another nail tech, sitting close by, doing a pedicure. *"She is asking too many questions."*

"Is this your first time at Perfect Nail?" The nail tech asked Ning, cutting off Ning's questions.

"Yes, it is."

"What do you do?"

"I work for my uncle," Ning replied, smiling.

The smiles dropped off the faces of the nail techs, like stones dropping into water. One minute the smiles were there, the next erased, unsure if there was a double meaning. The Vietnamese liked to drop double meanings all over the place. They considered it a sign of their superiority and intelligence, but hated it when it was done to them.

"I don't trust her," said the nail tech working next to Ning.

"Where are you from in Vietnam?" continued Ning.

"Saigon. I leave many years ago. Communists bad."

Another stock answer with a lie attached, thought Ning. Why were they all so nervous?

The door chimed and another customer came in.

"Look at this one, she's a big fish!" A nail tech said in reference to the new customer. *"Look at the diamonds on her fingers. She's rich."*

"She's mine," one of the male techs got up and moved towards the new customer, saying over his shoulder in Vietnamese, *"I like the ones with fake tits."*

"How do you know her poo taas are fake?" Said another Vietnamese male tech. There were two male technicians in this salon. From what Ning could understand, about the only thing they ever talked about was the customer's breasts.

"Look at them! No woman her age has tits like that," he said in Vietnamese, then switched to a big grin and pidgin English. "Hello. Is first time at Perfect Nails?" He led her away towards a pedicure chair.

The other nail techs seemed to shrink back from the men. Ning thought there must be a hierarchy and the men were at the top of it.

Or the girls were afraid of them.

"Yes, I think her mommas are fake," said one of the girl technicians.

The male technician looked up from his customer's feet, still smiling, and said to the girl in Vietnamese over his shoulder,

"Shut up you little crack whore or I'll tell Johnny Tran and he will strip the skin off your face with pliers."

The girls immediately fell silent. Ning watched as the girls seemed to almost freeze in their tracks, smiles now frozen on their face's.

Ning knew some Vietnamese were very superstitious, and this Johnny Tran seemed to be some sort of boogey man.

There was no doubt the girls feared him.

"I am the number-one Ninja, and I have killed
all the Shoguns in front of me."

Shaquille O'Neal

Chapter 6

It was generally agreed by all that knew him that Johnny Tran was completely psychotic.

Johnny was one of Lo Chin's enforcers, and he loved his work. Lo Chin was a Vietnamese Godfather. Lo Chin found Johnny in the slums of Hong Kong many years before. Johnny was also a Vietnamese immigrant, and a victim of Thai pirates. The difference was, the experience destroyed Johnny's mind.

Johnny loved all things Samurai. The Hong Kong film industry fed that love. Even Lo Chin had to admit that some of the tricks Johnny employed, although dramatic, actually worked. Johnny could sneak up on someone at night, be inches away, and be completely invisible when he wanted to be.

Johnny adopted the use of several Samurai weapons, including the katana (Long sword) and tanto (Short sword). He also owned a number of them. The short sword, he carried under his arm when wearing a business suit.

He planned his jobs with skill and precision, always leaving himself an escape route, which was probably why he was still alive. While Samurai skills could serve him well when sneaking up on a target, they wouldn't stop a bullet. A Samurai sword was no match for an automatic machine gun and he knew it.

Just because he was a sociopath didn't mean he was stupid.

Lo Chin remembered the first job he had hired Johnny to do. A rival gang leader cheated Lo Chin during a shipment of narcotics. Which of course, couldn't go unanswered.

"How can I be of service, Grandfather?" Johnny said, standing before his boss

"I have a business associate who is proving troublesome."

"You have but to command, Grandfather."

"I wish him to be taught a lesson. He will be traveling with two or more bodyguards. Is this a problem for you?" Lo Chin asked, already knowing the answer.

"It will be no problem. How severe is this lesson to be?"

"Dispose of the bodyguards as you will, but bring him to me…. alive"

"As you wish, Grandfather."

He gave Johnny a manila envelope with all the information he needed, including where, Wang Lee, the gang leader, would be two nights from then.

Lo Chin got to the rendezvous early wanting to see Johnny work. Johnny, of course, didn't know he was being watched. While Lo Chin didn't know Johnny would pick this spot, given the set of circumstances, it was the best place for an ambush. If Johnny was any good, he would know that too.

The alley was dark and Lo Chin never saw Johnny arrive. His opponent's bodyguards were also some of the best Hong Kong had to offer. If the ambush went sour, there was nothing to connect Johnny to Lo Chin, therefore, the blow back would be minimal. As usual, Lo Chin covered all his bases.

Wang Lee came out of the nightclub through the back door. First came a bodyguard, looking up and down the alley. Sensing and seeing no danger, he waved his boss out. Wang Lee had an underage girl beneath each arm and cradled a young breast in each hand. The second bodyguard took up the rear.

They almost made it to the car.

Johnny literally materialized out of nowhere, in back of the second bodyguard. Dressed in black, he swung the Japanese long sword directly horizontal of the bodyguard's spine. The katana sliced through muscle and bone with ease. The swinging motion carried him back into the shadows. By the time the bodyguard fell, Johnny was already invisible again. It left the bodyguard alive, but paralyzed for life.

The forward bodyguard, sensing danger, pulled a gun and rushed to his comrade's side, turning his back on his principle, but standing in front of him where he expected the attack to occur. Again, the katana came out of nowhere, first taking the gun hand off at the wrist, then a spinning movement, and the second strike severed his spinal column. It took literally seconds, and the number two bodyguard was down, and Johnny was back in the shadows.

The girls started to scream then, seeing the two men down, with their torsos moving independently of each other as muscle spasms raked their bodies, yet unable to move. Wang Lee cuffed one girl to shut her up, then tossed her aside. He then grabbed the other girl, put a gun to her head, and pulled her close to use as a human shield.

Blood from the two bodyguards ran as separate trickles, joined together, then ran as one toward Wang Lee's thousand dollar Italian shoes. The girl with her head forced down saw and tried to move out of the way of the blood tide. Wang looked down as she was trying to squirm away, and that was all it took.

Johnny, once again appearing out of nowhere in a swirling, black ballet, cut through the girl right under the rib cage, and swirled back into the darkness before Wang could even get a shot off. Wang noticed the girl had suddenly got lighter, as the lower half of her torso separated cleanly from her body, and he felt the warm weight of spilling intestines and gore all over his shoes.

Wang threw down the bisected corpse of the girl and turned, making a run for the driver's side door, planning to make a quick getaway. He made it as far as the door when Johnny, now underneath the car, severed both hamstrings at the heels. Wang Lee went down, his feet no longer obeying the commands of his legs. Wang bounced off the car door, and fell to the asphalt street, looking directly under the car and straight into Johnny's mad eyes.

Johnny rolled out from under the car gracefully, ignoring the second girl whimpering in fright, holding her head down. He stood over Wang Lee. Lee tried to make a grab for his gun, but Johnny speared him through the hand before he could reach it, then kicked the gun away.

Johnny took his time opening the trunk of the luxury car, and picking Wang up under the arms dragged him to the trunk and folded him into it. He closed the trunk, and with a flash of his katana took the whimpering girl's head off at the shoulders, so there would be no witnesses. He then went to the driver's side, got in, and drove away.

Lo Chin looked at his watch. No more than two minutes from start to finish. He nodded his head with satisfaction. He saw big things ahead in Johnny's future.

Eventually, he gave Johnny Tran the Des Moines operation, the largest South of Chicago.

"It is sometimes an appropriate response to reality to go insane."

Phillip K. Dick

Chapter 7

Johnny Tran absently picked a stubborn piece of dead hooker from between his back molars with a wooden toothpick.

Johnny didn't feel a thing as he fed the two lifeless girls into the industrial sized meat grinder at the back the restaurant.

He used a stick to press the body parts into the churning metal rollers. He marveled that American engineering could even grind up human bones with ease.

Johnny Tran, a Vietnamese gangster, learned his trade from Thai pirates when his family had to flee Vietnam in 1988.

Johnny Tran's family fled Vietnam on 27 November, 1988, because they were Chinese and were told to leave. He remembered that the Communist government made them leave all of their belongings and property behind. They had to pay for each person's passage, and the authorities saw to it that the boats were overcrowded and not sea worthy. He was part of a huge exodus of Chinese refugees that day, marching to an uncertain fate.

He was seven years old.

The journey took 14 days and 15 nights, in a boat that was built to only hold about 20, but instead held 278. The conditions were deplorable. People were packed in like sardines. People vomited on themselves, as there was absolutely no room for movement. They were given no food or navigation equipment.

Johnny Tran booked a passage out of Vietnam with his mother, father, brother, and younger sister. After several days at sea, the boat was stranded and without food or water. They were attacked by pirates, who shot his brother. An old man's gold teeth were ripped out of his mouth with pliers, and a woman's baby was thrown into the sea because it cried from hunger.

The women were lined up, and a number of girls were selected, including his sister, and taken on board a fishing boat. Over the next week, the girls were repeatedly raped. One of the girls could not stand it, and in the end, the pirates couldn't stand her. She was thrown over-board. Another was sold to a village brothel - "The Paradise Massage Parlor." Johnny met her many years later in Hong Kong and found out she became pregnant, but the baby was aborted with a bamboo stick. Eventually, she escaped and was handed over to the UN.

Some of the women and children were transferred to the boats and never heard of again. The men were kept in the hold and brought up one by one to be clubbed to death for sport. Eventually, the refugees panicked and tried to rush the pirates. The pirates, in anger, rammed the boat to sink it. Some refugees managed to escape but were pushed under water with poles. Thirteen survivors managed to escape by swimming away under cover of darkness.

A few days later, seven pirates armed with guns, knives, and ham-mers attacked the 129 Vietnamese left alive on the boat. The women were, once again, raped.

The pirates then turned on a petite 16 year old virgin and began to rape her as her father looked on. Unable to accommodate their bru-tality, the girl began to hemorrhage. As she slowly bled to death, they continued to rape her. After she died, they covered the upper half of her body with a sheet and raped her some more.

By the time the pirates were finished with the girl, her father's eyes had seen more horror than his mind could handle. He went insane, along with young Johnny Tran.

The passengers were stripped of any valuables. The attractive girls were spared only to be sold into prostitution in Thailand. What was left of his family survived by clinging to a raft made of three bloated corps-es until rescued by another boat of refugees.

They arrived on Koh Phi's shore in Thailand on 15 December, 1988.

The survivors were made to strip and then landed on the beach, and their boat was sunk. The captain of the boat purposefully caused it to sink a short distance from shore, because he knew that other boats had been forced to turn around and go back – many of them perishing at sea. Others were attacked by Thai pirates yet again.

He recalled his father carrying him to shore on his shoulders while holding his mother's hand – the water coming up to their chins. As they were wading to the shore, there were about five hundred Thais waiting for them on the beach, with rocks in their hands who then proceeded to pelt the refugees as they made their way to the shore. Johnny Tran vividly recalled the sounds that the rocks made as they came into contact with flesh. All he could do was to reach up and cover his head as they were still making their way out of the water. He recalled seeing Thai police officers that stood by and watched the whole thing transpire, doing nothing to stop it. He was the only child that survived.

He remembered the black market of the refugee camp and how the refugees were mercilessly exploited. A small bag of rice cost fifty dollars. A pot to cook it in – one hundred dollars. You had to build your own shelter. His father told him how he was reduced to tears when he couldn't afford to purchase an apple for his child to eat.

Johnny Tran was at the refugee camp for a little over six months before he was sponsored to Hong Kong. It was there he met Lo Chin. Eventually, through the Refugee Settlement Program, he came to the United States. After gaining American citizenship, he went back to Vietnam under a different name as a Chinese business man from Hong Kong in 2005, when the Communist government decided they really liked Chinese's business (And the money it generated within the economy) after all.

To say that Johnny Tran had an ax to grind with Thai's and Vietnamese was an understatement.

Johnny Tran always heard revenge was a dish best served cold. By age thirty-three, Johnny Tran had been feasting for almost twenty-five years.

"Cannibals prefer those who have no spines."

Stanislaw Lem

Chapter 8

Wang Lee, looked up at Johnny Tran as he lay in the trunk, and had no doubt he was going to die. It was only a question of how badly.

Johnny Tran backed Wang Lee's car into the basement of a restaurant in the China Town district of Saigon. He opened the trunk and stared down at Wang Lee, he felt no pity, no mercy, he felt nothing at all.

Tran duct-taped Wang Lee's hands together in front of him at the wrist, then taped his feet. Since his ham strings had been cut, his feet were difficult to work with as they flopped all over the place, but he got the job done.

Once finished he called some soldiers over, and they hauled Wang Lee out of the trunk and hauled him over to a metal table. The duct tape handcuffs were cut off then, and each arm and leg, was fastened to a table leg. Wang Lee was spread eagled on the table. The soldiers then cut off every stitch of clothing so that he was naked.

"Did you think I would not know, or that I wouldn't find out it was you?" Lo Chin asked, stepping into Wang's line of vision.

"Truthfully, I did not care either way," said Wang, not showing the least fear.

"I commend you on your honesty. You are now at the end of your life. So we can talk frankly, as one man to another."

"I intend to talk to you in that fashion anyway. While my life might end tonight, your end is also not that far off."

"That possibility has never been far from my existence, and I came to peace with it years ago. Like you, I don't fear my death. So let it come. Nevertheless, tonight you are the guest of honor. What I want to know is who betrayed me."

"You think that I will tell you?"

"I know that you will tell me."

Lo Chin snapped his fingers, and a powerful light was brought to the table. Wang Lee could hear the clatter of metal instruments being loaded on a hand table and the screech of unoiled wheels as it bumped across the uneven concrete floor. Next, his arms were loosed and a large wooden wedge was inserted under his back so that he was in a semi-reclining position, able to look down on his body.

"You knew the time and place of the pick up point, as well as who the courier was going to be when he came off the plane from Macao. This means you were tipped off on the Chinese side. This means I have a traitor in my organization, and I want to know who it is."

Wang Lee started to laugh then. Not the laugh of a man afraid to die, or the laugh of hysteria. But the laugh of someone finding something truly funny.

"You find the situation you are in amusing?" Lo Chin asked.

"As a matter of fact, I do. What if I don't know the answer to your question?"

"Then, of course, I wouldn't believe you. You will die anyway, but I can make it quick instead of long and drawn out. The choice is yours."

"I will tell you the truth. I have nothing to fear, and nothing to lose. Please go back to your ancestral home in An Giang province and fuck your mother. Yes, I know who you are and where you are from. Your family comes from a long line of inbred monsters and the Communists were right to get rid of you and your family the first chance they got."

Johnny Tran stepped forward then. He took a scalpel off the table, and made an incision on the back and side of Wang's midriff. Dropping the scalpel on the table, he reached inside the incision and using foreceps, clamped off the renal artery and vein on one side of a kidney, and the ureter on the other side. Picking up the scalpel again, he cut the kidney free and brought it out, laying it in a stainless steel dish. Wang Lee was forced to watch his own body being dissected.

"Still nothing to say?" asked Lo Chin. "Usually, we wait until your body is dead, then sell your organs."

Wang Lee wouldn't give Lo Chin the satisfaction of even a grunt of pain. Instead, he silently passed out.

Lo Chin was impressed. Normally someone witnessing their own body being carved up was instantly reduced to gibbering and guttural howls. Johnny Tran stepped forward once again. Crudely, but expertly, he sewed up the incision. He poured water on Wang's face and slapped him awake.

Making sure he was in Wang's line of vision, Johnny Tran picked up the kidney from the dish and started eating it in front of Wang. He held it in both hands, taking large bites out of it. Blood trickled from each corner of his mouth.

Wang's last sight on this earth was watching Johnny Tran in the depths of his insanity. He died, quietly and silently, without saying a word.

"What do you want us to do with his body," asked Johnny Tran.

"The meat shipment isn't until next week and we are low on beef, " said Lo Chin, "Some of him can be used to make Bun Bao, the thighs and buttocks, slice thinly for use in Bun Bo Hue. The rest of him can be ground up and used to make sausage."

Lo Chin's customers had regularly remarked that his specialties, always seemed fresher and tastier than Vietnamese beef, especially the Pho.

"What's your secret?" many asked.

"It is what you feed the cattle that makes them special," he always replied.

"I only follow one party: the Vietnamese party."

Ho Chi Minh

Chapter 9

Flynn had no doubt the Vietnamese played hard.

During Flynn's tenure on the police force, the Vietnamese gangs were relatively quiet and low-key. When gang violence did flare up, it was confined to the Vietnamese gangs or the Vietnamese community themselves. The gangs preyed on their own kind.

The Vietnamese community itself offered no help. None would talk to the police, or any outsider. Not that he blamed them. In this way, the Vietnamese Mafia could maintain total control over the community.

The police didn't prevent crime anymore. The police were the urban janitors who cleaned up the mess afterwards. For all the high-tech computers, crime labs, DNA databases, and fictional 'reality' shows, the truth was, if a snitch didn't tell them what was going down, and where, the modern police detective rarely got up from his desk.

That was the big secret the police industrial complex didn't want anyone to know. Their propaganda machine spit out daily doses of how efficient they were. In reality, if no one tattled, nothing ever happened. So they extolled the virtues of technology but in reality paid off informants big bucks made from "civil forfeitures."

Flynn had to get a feel for who he was dealing with. That meant surveillance. Surveillance meant mind-numbing boredom watching nothing for hours on end. Luckily, Flynn bought a used yellow taxi through his connections so at least he could do it in relative comfort. 4G and a cell phone usually meant he could run his business at the same time as well. Flynn settled in.

According to Lamar, the Vietnamese were running a prostitution ring as well as drugs from restaurants, and nail shops all over the city. Word was; one of the enforcers was named Johnny Tran, who was certifiable and carried a Samurai sword.

Flynn grunted. Probably an idiot. It ought to make him easy to spot anyway. There was also someone above him who called the shots but details were sketchy.

The story on the street was that the drugs and girls were run only by lieutenants who had to know the passwords, which were changed daily. The lieutenants dealt with the mid-level dealers and pimps. Nothing ever reached above street level making the arrest of the bosses nearly impossible.

Flynn set up surveillance a couple of blocks away from the "Dac Biet Restaurant" in an alley, and watched the back entrance. He saw nothing but the usual coming and goings of a busy restaurant. The next night he chose another restaurant. Still nothing and he was running out of time. He tried a nail shop the next day.

He saw a striking Vietnamese male walk into "Perfect Nails Spa" wearing Armani and could tell by the bulge under his suit coat, and the way he was carrying himself, he was concealing a weapon. What was most striking about him was the Samurai hairdo. The top of his head was shaved with a long ponytail hanging down his back. Flynn's Canon EOS digital camera clicked away continuously and formed almost a video of stills, which in turn fed the images simultaneously to his laptop. Facial recognition software on his laptop, linked into a private database for private investigators immediately fed his features through national arrest records, which were public record. No arrests on record.

Back in the day, when he had a badge, he would have accosted him and asked to see a concealed weapons permit. A faintly illegal tactic which wouldn't hold up in court, but would also be overlooked if he came up with any outstanding felony warrants. It was a chicken-shit cop tactic, but still could yield valuable information in the right situation. The fact was, the weapon probably wasn't illegal. A person could legally carry a weapon anywhere he wanted with a permit, but it would give Flynn a chance to size up his opponent under stress.

However, he didn't have a badge anymore. So he had to be content with just watching the outside of the building.

Johnny Tran walked into the Perfect Nails Spa on University Ave. and entered a beehive of activity. All fifteen nails stations were occupied. Voices in two different languages babbled constantly over the whine of nail buffers and loud, sucking sounds of draining pedicure chairs. The air smelled faintly medicinal, of acetone and Jasmine.

The vocal racket dropped an octave when he entered. The Vietnamese fell silent. He walked straight through to the back of the spa. It probably didn't register on the radar of any of the American women that an armed man had just entered the premises. He entered an office at the back.

"Your weekly 'gift' to the Godfather is ten thousand dollars a week. You were short five thousand last week, which means this week you owe twenty thousand, including interest. You are no doubt anxious to pay your debt," Johnny Tran said the owner.

"Business has not been good…" the owner whined softly, hoping to catch a break.

"I understand," Johnny Tran said. "Perhaps then you're interested in alternate payment arrangements?"

"No, no…I didn't mean I don't have the money. I will happily pay what I owe, of course."

Johnny Tran noted with satisfaction the owner had a hard time counting out the twenty thousand dollars with one of his little fingers already missing. The stump was healing up quite nicely since he sliced it off last week.

"Alternate Payment arrangements" were usually painful when Johnny Tran was the banker.

Once the money and accounting were up to date, Johnny said, "I hear one of your girls has a big mouth. Which one is it?"

"They are girls. They all have big mouths."

Johnny pulled his tanto halfway from its sheath under his jacket in threat. The owner paled.

"It was Tuyet."

"Have her finish with her customer and come back here quietly," Johnny said softly.

Flynn watched the nail spa for twelve uneventful hours. He never saw Johnny Tran leave the spa out the back, quickly and silently, forcing a scared girl into a dirty white van.

He did, however, see a beautiful Asian girl exit the nail salon from the front, and waving her hand in the Asian fashion, palm down, flag his taxi.

"When you understand your obligations as a man,
then you can understand your obligations to society."

H. Rap Brown

Chapter 10

She was absolutely stunning.

Flynn rolled up in his yellow taxi. She was so beautiful; he even got
out and opened the door for her, all thoughts of the surveillance forgotten. Flynn got back in the front, and adjusted his rear-view mirror
so he could look at her dark eyes.

"Where to?"

"Would you mind just heading in the direction of downtown? I
need some time to think," Ning said.

A definite foreign accent, thought Flynn. It made her even more
exotic.

"No problem."

Flynn studied her in the rear-view mirror as he rolled away from
the nail shop. She was looking down at her nails, not altogether
pleased with what she saw.

"So what was with the guy with the strange hairdo I saw entering
the shop earlier?"

Ning looked up and stared at Flynn's eye reflection in the mirror.

"Good question. I was just wondering that myself."

"So you aren't a regular there?"

"Heavens no. I just needed a quick touch up before a business
meeting."

"Really? What do you do?"

"I'm a VP at Cobalt Industries."

Flynn felt a familiar sensation. It came as a soft tingling in the pit of his stomach. It signaled that something drew the attention of his ghost, Flynn's mentor. A calmness flooded into Flynn's being, and he knew his teacher was sitting beside him.

"Who owns Cobalt Industries?"

"Max Cobalt. You know him?" Ning asked.

The feeling in the pit of his stomach was more intense now. The 'small voice' was going to be speaking soon.

"I've heard of him. I don't know him. What's he like? A good boss?"

"Max is…different."

Who is he? Flynn said into his mind to his ghost.

He's my son, came the reply.

At that moment, unbidden, an image came into Flynn's mind. Almost like a hallucination in its intensity. The flashback was in Technicolor…

Both James Cobalt and Flynn were standing in Jeffery Prescott's study, moments before Cobalt died.

James Cobalt looked at Flynn. "You owe me."

"You saved my life in order to ask me to take yours?"

"Yes, I did. Because I saw a man of honor."

"As a man of honor, I refuse."

"I understand," James Cobalt said quietly, "Then I ask this. Extend my debt to Mia and my children. Whatever they want, whatever they need, anytime, anywhere, for the rest of your life."

"That I can do." Flynn said quietly, meaning it.

"You can drop me off at 801 Grand Avenue. Max has a penthouse there," Ning said, causing the image in Flynn's mind to shatter, like broken glass, collapsing inward into a thousand pieces.

"OK. So, what is it you guys do? Buy businesses, and take them over and run them into the ground for profit?"

Ning laughed. It sounded like wind chimes tinkling in a soft breeze. Flynn was totally enchanted.

"Hardly. It's more like we find ailing businesses, usually because of bad management, inject needed capital into them and make them viable again. Max is very good at spotting them. I'm very good at negotiating with the owners. We make a good team."

I bet you do, thought Flynn, *I bet Max Cobalt is real close to his 'team members' too.*

Flynn lifted his eyes to the rear-view mirror and saw Ning staring right at him, reading his mind.

"It's not like that. Max is a professional," Ning said coolly. "You know there is a possibility I was hired because of my own talents and abilities."

Flynn took his hands off the wheel momentarily and held them up in surrender.

"I wasn't trying to imply anything, Ma'am." Switching subjects quickly, Flynn said, "Did you get the feeling something was off back at that nail salon?"

"You mean besides the fact that a Samurai not belonging to this century entered? He wasn't there for a pedicure, if that was what you mean."

Flynn smiled, liking her sense of humor.

"What did he want?"

"I don't know. He just walked into the back, like he owned the place. A little while later one of the girls walked back too. She was scared shitless, I can tell you that."

"Where are you from?"

"Thailand."

"Are all Thai girls as beautiful as you?"

"A lot of them are."

"What's your name?"

"Ning."

"Is that your first name, or last name?"

"Both."

"I think Max Cobalt is a pretty lucky guy."

Ning smiled and said nothing, acknowledging the compliment with silence. Flynn weaved his way through traffic to 801 Grand Avenue, the tallest skyscraper downtown.

"Lucky doesn't even begin to describe Max Cobalt," Ning said, getting out of the cab, and handing Flynn a hundred dollar bill for a twenty dollar cab ride. "I like you. I hope we meet again," she said, as she got out of the cab and disappeared through the brass doors of 801 Grand Avenue.

"Childhood sometimes does pay a second visit to man, youth never."

Anna Jameson

Chapter 11

Max Cobalt was the CEO of Cobalt Industries. He was a Corporate Predator. He looked for, then bought, companies which he had an interest in. He then installed his own management team, and after that went on the prowl for more companies to conquer. It was an adversarial and cut-throat occupation. More than once he received death threats, and a few instances of people trying to make good on them.

Ning came from Thailand three months before, in the US on a Tourist visa. She had to go to Immigration in a few days and formally apply for her H1B Work Visa. She had met Cobalt when the two did a job together a few months back flying a field hospital to Three Pagoda Pass. Since Cobalt owed her one, she and her door gunner, Wee, thought it might be time for a change of pace and showed up on Cobalt's doorstep. Especially since both were looking at jail time back in Thailand.

"I didn't get to see either of you before I left Thailand. I tried, but Poo wouldn't give me your number," Cobalt said to Ning standing on his doorstep months before.

Cobalt looked at Wee. Wee, playing a joke as usual, had stolen a pizza delivery car and shown up on his doorstep with a hot pizza and a ridiculous uniform.

"Wee, good to see you. Do you still want a tip?"

"Sure. I am a lowly immigrant in a strange country," Wee said, smiling.

"Here's your tip. Get a new uniform, you look ridiculous."

Wee laughed. "You going to invite us in? Ha! Impolite, Americans!"

"It depends; do I get to eat the pizza?"

"Yes, Poo can be over protective at times," said Ning, switching the subject back.

"Tell me about it. Yes, please, come in."

Cobalt led them to the dining room. Ning and Wee walked in, looking around, eyes wide. He took the pizza from Wee, opened the box, and took a slice. The Thais helped themselves as well.

"Where did you get the car?" Cobalt asked.

"Wee stole it. Hot wiring he learned from his misspent youth in Thailand."

"Well, you can't leave a stolen car in my driveway. The pizza is from down the street. You'll have to return it and leave it there."

"Yeah, okay, no problem," Wee said, not too concerned.

Wee spied the home theater system and immediately bee lined towards it, pizza and Cobalt forgotten. He picked up the remote, turned it on, then flicked through the channels like he knew what he was looking for. He stopped on the Cartoon Network, sat down on the leather couch, and started watching SpongeBob SquarePants.

Ning sighed. "He's an asshole, but he grows on you," looking towards Wee.

"How did you find me? Not even my friends know where I live."

"I have news for you, Cobalt. You don't have any friends."

"They are getting rather hard to come by."

"It wasn't that difficult. You just need to know where to look, or who to ask."

"How long are you here for? Are you even in the US legally?"

"Of course. Your government is very generous to Thai people."

"I owe you both from Three Pagoda Pass. Without you, I wouldn't have survived. I don't forget my debts."

"Your debt is paid. But I was serious. If we are to stay here, we need jobs, green cards, and visas."

"The jobs are the easy part. Green cards and visa are a bit more difficult," said Cobalt.

"How difficult? We have money if you need to pay anyone off."

"No, that won't work here. I need time, maybe two weeks, maybe a month."

"Then I'm glad I'm here to make your life interesting," said Ning, smiling. "My immigration interview is in one week."

"Whenever I start feeling too arrogant about myself, I always take a trip to the U.S. The immigration guys kick the star out of my stardom."

Shahrukh Khan

Chapter 12

The Immigration officer came from behind bullet-proof glass, through an explosion-proof door, and called out a name, haltingly,..."Veep-pa-daa…"

Ning stood up, "That would be me."

"I'm sorry, I can't pronounce your name." He stood looking Ning up and down, as she walked towards him, clearly impressed with her beauty.

"No problem. Americans have a hard time with it. You can call me Ning."

"How do you say it?"

" Wi-pa-da, Road-ya-na-suk-chai

"Is that your first name or last name?"

Ning sighed. "Both. Just call me Ning, it is easier."

"OK, my name is James Marshall. I'll be conducting your interview."

They walked down a long hallway, row after row of small offices on both sides of the corridor. Windows started waist high and went up to the ceiling, so that each office could be viewed from the exterior hallway. Ning also noticed the video cameras at both ends of the corridor and in some of the interview rooms as well. Some of the offices were occupied. Others were empty. The hall was clean, the floor highly buffed and polished. It smelled of pine scented cleaner. Small laminated name plaques which could be slid in and out, with the changing of the office's occupiers, were beside each door. Half-way down they entered one that said, "J. Marshall, Interviewer."

James Marshall held out his hand, waist high, palm up, in a 'please enter first' gesture. Ning entered the small, bare office and sat down. Marshall entered after, and sat behind the desk. The office was devoid of any personal knickknacks or family photographs of any kind. No prints on the walls. It had a computer with a monitor on the desk turned away from her. It was an office made to be taken over by anyone, at anytime.

Marshall took out some reading glasses, wiped the lenses with his tie, and put them on. He tapped a key on the keyboard, and read from the screen.

"It's rather unusual for us to get an H1B visa application. Usually, those are handled at a consulate overseas."

"Well, it is an unusual situation."

"I see your occupation is listed as 'Budget and Management Systems Analysis'."

"Yes."

"That is a rather vague classification, Ms. Ning. Can you tell me what you do?"

"Yes, I'm Vice President of Acquisitions at Cobalt Industries."

"I see. What does Cobalt Industries like to acquire?"

"Usually other companies."

"Mr. Cobalt has thoughtfully provided all the necessary paperwork. Even a letter from the Secretary of State. He's got friends in high places. So this is more of a formality than anything. What was your job in Thailand?"

"I was a helicopter pilot with the Thai Military."

"And your Thai Military helicopter training prepared you for being a,"-glancing at the computer screen- "Budget and Management Systems Analyst?"

Before Ning could respond, another man stepped into the room. Marshall glanced up, but didn't introduce him. He sat in the second chair, and moved it so he could look directly at Ning. She smiled at him casually. His face revealed nothing, but his manner and bearing reeked of military or CIA.

"You were saying…?"

"Could you repeat the question, please?"

The mystery man spoke for the first time. "He was asking how a Thai helicopter pilot, possibly involved in dozens of murders at an illegal organ harvesting operation at Three Pagoda Pass in Burma, was allowed entry into the USA. Sorry if I jumped into your show, Jim."

Marshall waved the formality away with one hand. Both sets of eyes stared hard at Ning.

"Very simple. I was ordered to do a job by my government, and I did it."

"And your job was?"

"To fly two cargo containers to Three Pagoda Pass."

"Do you know what was in the containers?"

"Field hospitals was my understanding."

"I see. Something else I'm curious about."

He spread photographs of various Thai forms out on the desk, along with English translations, in front of Ning. One was a copy of Ning's passport, another a Thai birth certificate.

"In all these documents, you are a male. Yet clearly, that isn't the case. Can you explain?"

"Certainly, I'm transgendered." Ning said this openly, without a trace of embarrassment.

"You didn't think to tell the authorities that?"

"Of course not. Why should I?"

"Well it is deceptive, to say the least."

"How so? Your form asks my gender. I gave my gender truthfully. I am female. I didn't lie; I do not perjure. Would you like to see inside my panties?"

Both men secretly wanted to find out exactly what was in her panties.

"Yes, but you were born a male."

"You were born a baby. Are you still one now?"

"I'm asking the questions here," said the Spook.

"And I'm answering them."

Both men were clearly uncomfortable. They came into the meeting fully expecting to catch Ning in a lie, thereby voiding her application on the grounds of perjury, or failure to cooperate. They couldn't prove her account of Three Pagoda Pass was false, as the Thai military wasn't going to cooperate with Homeland Security over such a matter, and they had been warned off by some very high power.

"Just don't go there," the Spook's boss had said. Which, of course, only made the Spook more curious.

Since Ning wasn't lying about her gender, nor concealing it, and they had no way of proving it short of a strip search, which still wouldn't prove she was lying; they were left with their proverbial dicks in their hands.

Worse, they had the unsettling feeling she knew it. They weren't used to not being in control. The fact that she was more beautiful than 99% of American women also left them unsettled.

"I'm considering keeping you here indefinitely until we get to the bottom of this," said the Spook.

"Get to the 'bottom' of what?"

"I don't believe you. I think you're lying."

"You're entitled to your opinion."

"Answer my question!"

"Was there a question in your last two statements?"

Ning stayed silent then, looking both men in the eye. "Your job must be a difficult one," said Ning, finally.

"Oh?"

"Yes, you see people coming in here everyday, scraping and groveling, the flotsam and jetsam of humanity, all yearning to be free."

"Your point?"

"It's just that in your job, you never know who you're dealing with. For example, I could be the daughter of a high placed Thai government official. One who knows and plays golf with your bosses, even your boss's bosses. Many times up the food chain from you. Which means your position is very precarious. A misstep, with the wrong person, could end your career. Especially when there is the possible appearance of discrimination, or gender bias. I believe on the application form I signed it says to report any instances of gender bias if encountered. Since Max Cobalt, judging by the letter in your hand, has the ear of the Secretary of State, it makes your position precarious. I'm going to take a wild guess and say the Secretary of State is above your pay grade."

Both men were looking at each other now.

"I can assure you…"

"Or maybe you're homophobic. What is it you Americans like to say… 'Don't ask, don't tell?'" Ning crossed her long, shapely legs, staring at each man in turn. "When all the paperwork is in order, duly signed and stamped by the correct people, and you have to make a 'judgment call' it must be challenging. Especially a judgment call which could have such serious repercussions to a person's career, which is the reason why I say, your job must be a difficult one."

The silence carried for longer than it should have as both men suddenly didn't seem to want to meet Ning's eyes. They understood the veiled threat completely.

The little bitch nailed the situation correctly.

"You'll find your passport, stamped with a ten-year H1B visa, along with a Social Security card at the reception desk when you leave," said the Spook, looking at the ceiling.

Ning smiled politely to both men as she got up to leave.

"You're Thai Intelligence, aren't you?" The Spook asked.

"I'm an intelligent Thai, yes, if that's what you mean."

"Bureaucracy, the rule of no one,
has become the modern form of despotism."

Mary McCarthy

Chapter 13

If Ning attacked their intelligence, Wee, Ning's door gunner, and Max Cobalt's bodyguard, decided to assault Homeland Security's idea of absurdity.

Wee was dressed in a two thousand dollar pin striped business suit. He wore a pressed white linen shirt. His power tie, dark blue, was knotted in a Windsor; the creases in his navy blue pants knife sharp.

He also wore a yellow and black stripped beanie on his head with a propeller on top, spinning in the air-conditioned breeze.

His lawyer sitting with him, wasn't amused.

They sat in the same Homeland Security waiting room Ning had been in the day before.

With nothing better to do, Wee thought about the vagaries of life and about how he came to be sitting here...

Wee was also with Captain Ning on the ill-fated mission to Three Pagoda Pass. His Captain had been under strict orders from the Thai High Command, not to fire on the Burmese, as it could be considered an act of war on the part of Thailand. Those orders were duly passed down from his Captain to himself. But when it came time to protect his Captain and his aircraft, he did what any self-respecting door gunner would do...he blew the shit out of whatever threat came within range.

He would happily do so again. He admitted as much in front of the Thai Military Tribunal, who sentenced him to seven years hard labor for insubordination and disobeying a direct order.

He would have served his time. He knew he disobeyed an order. How-

ever, when the choice is allowing someone to hurt his Captain or remov-ing the threat, his karma was clear.

Mai pen lui.

That was until Captain Ning showed up at the military jail, in full uniform. Captain bars shining, her combat service ribbons gleaming.

"I'm here to see Sergeant Wee. Can you please escort him to the visitor's area?"

The Chief of Staff at the prison examined her papers, nodded, and buzzed her through the door. If any of the jail orderlies thought about giv-ing her a hard time, her smile was enough to disarm them.

Captain Ning was nothing if not drop-dead gorgeous.

"Sergeant Wee, —— —- to the visitor's area. You —- a visitor." The intercom was old, and frequently cut in and out, losing one word or an-other.

Ning looked around the visitor's area. It was depressing. Gray, cinder-block walls with peeling paint. Dirty windows high up in the wall, with chicken-wire reinforced glass let feeble light into the room. It smelled of desperation, disinfectant, and hopelessness.

After some minutes, Wee appeared in prison orange, his feet and hands shackled.

"Take the leg irons and handcuffs off this man immediately," Ning said to the orderly.

"My orders are they stay on, Ma'am," the orderly said.

"Then you better take a quick look at the bars on my shoulders, and the service ribbons on my chest, and decide which orders you are going to obey."

The orderly was only too happy to look at Ning's chest.

The leg irons and handcuffs came off.

Once they were alone, Wee didn't offer his usual idiotic smile.

"Sawadee Khrap Captain. It is good to see you. But you put your career at risk coming to see me."

"You mean the same way you put your career at risk to save mine?"

"That was different, Captain. You owe me nothing. I did my job, that's all."

"As I'm doing mine, Khun Wee."

"Sergeant?" Ning said to the Duty Officer, "This man's mother is dy-ing, and I have full responsibility for transporting him to the hospital. The papers are with the supervising duty officer. I want him ready to go in fifteen minutes."

Wee's eyes widened. "My mother? What happened to my mother?"

Instead of going to the hospital, they went to a private military air-base in Korat. Ning had rented a private jet with the money Cobalt had left her after the job at Three Pagoda Pass.

As happens in Thailand, people are paid, and their passports are stamped with the appropriate stamps allowing entry into the US.

Wee bounced up and down on the Corinthian leather seats all the way across the Pacific, grinning like a fool, and drinking champagne. Being a private jet, as long as their papers were in order they by-passed the usual dog and pony show reserved for the unwashed masses at Immigration.

They got to the US and Wee, grinning the whole time, promptly stole a pizza delivery car left running in some fool's driveway, showing up on Cobalt's doorstep hours later.

"War-a-whatsit…" James Marshall, was thoroughly sick of trying to pronounce Thai names.

Wee stood up, as did his lawyer.

"Please state your name for the record?"

"Worrawut Wattanasin," said the lawyer.

"Does he have a nick-name?" Marshall asked, as he led them down the same corridor as Ning the day before, into the same office.

"Yes, you can call him Wee."

"Does he speak English? Are you his interpreter?"

"No, I'm his lawyer."

"I see. Why does he need a lawyer?"

"I guess to do his interpreting."

This gave Marshall his first chance to examine Wee. He wasn't impressed either. Wee stood there grinning like an idiot on acid yellow beanie lighting up the room and propeller spinning. Even Marshall was having a problem keeping a straight face, so he decided to direct his questions at his lawyer.

"I see he is also looking for an H1B visa, sponsored by Cobalt Industries…" The statement came out as a question.

"Yes, he is," answered the lawyer.

"Cobalt Industries seems to be hiring a lot of Thais lately…"

"Is that a statement or a question?"

"Which would you like it to be?"

"Well then, if you have no more questions, we'll be going," said

Wee's lawyer, preparing to stand.

"Relax, we're just getting started. I have plenty of questions. Here's the first one; does your client speak English?"

"Like many Asians he understands it better than he speaks it."

"I see. Is that a yes, or a no?"

"That's neither yes, nor no."

"I see." He looked directly at Wee, and raised his voice, drawing out his words, so the mentally challenged could understand, "Do-you-understand-English?"

Wee could speak perfectly good English. However, there was no sense in letting Homeland Security know that since it gave him an advantage. So his smile grew even bigger, and he said by rote,

"You order pizza? $15.99. Don't forget tip!"

Marshall looked at the Lawyer, "What is he talking about?"

The lawyer shrugged, "You asked the question."

As if on cue, once again, the Spook showed up. This time he had a hard time squeezing into the small office, bumping into Wee, and the lawyer as he made his way the best he could to a corner, by Marshall.

"I was wondering when the CIA was going to show up, or is it DoD?" asked the lawyer.

"It's neither. Shall we dispense with the bullshit and you can tell us what you know about Three Pagoda Pass."

"I know it's a popular tourist destination in Thailand. The "Bridge Over the River Kwai'" and all. I know 90,000 Allied POWs died there during World War Two and…"

"And I bet Little Wee-Wee here knows all about the organ harvesting operation."

"Do they have a class at Langley called Offensive and Petty 101?"

"Could you ask him?"

"If they have a class at Langley called…"

"If he knows anything about the organ harvesting operation at Three Pagoda Pass, and specifically Richard Jenkins role in it."

The lawyer leaned over and whispered in Wee's ear. Wee listened intently, nodding his head up and down vigorously, held up his right hand in an I-swear-to-tell-the-truth-and-nothing-but-the-truth gesture, thought for a moment, then leaned back into his lawyer's ear, speaking rapidly in Thai for several long minutes.

Wee gestured wildly, and made chopping motions with his hands.

Then pantomimed holding a large fire hose, spraying a raging inferno.

"Well?" Both men leaned in, not to miss a word.

"He says, he has go wee-wee."

"They may use my body but my mind is free. In my mind I escape."

Gladys Lawson,

Chapter 14

The men were from Southern China, and they wanted to buy wives.

Johnny Tran sat in Lo Chin's office in the Go Vap District of Ho Chi Minh City. Johnny made trips between Saigon and Des Moines, Iowa every month procuring new merchandise. The office was located upstairs from one of Lo Chin's busy restaurants.

Lo Chin was Johnny Tran's boss and head of the Vietnamese Mafia.

Of course, very few people knew that, and Lo Chin certainly didn't look the part. He looked like the simple restaurant owner he was. He was 55ish, with a pot belly, going bald on top, and he chain smoked. He owned a seafood restaurant in the Go Vap district of Saigon, as well as others scattered around the city. Lo Chin was originally from Vietnam. He fled Vietnam in the late 1970's escaping the Communist takeover. He returned with a different name and passport in 1995, and gradually built up his fearsome reputation and empire here. Lo Chin was one of the younger "Grandfathers."

There were a number of half eaten dishes of various local recipes sitting on a low table. Southern Chinese are partial to dog, so there were a number of dog meat dishes.

During the meal, girls came into Lo Chin's office bringing dishes laden with food, and carried out empty plates. Johnny made sure these were some of his most desirable. The girls wore short skirts with no panties and see-through tops. The brothers were clearly impressed and were encouraged to examine the merchandise. They ran their dirty fin-

gernails up the inside of soft thighs, many times provoking an unconscious shudder of revulsion from the girls.

The men, two brothers, came from a fishing village on the southern
coast of China. They had a hard life, were greasy looking, and had the
smell of fish ground into their clothes and pores. They picked up the
shredded dog meat with chopsticks held in dirty hands. Lo Chin knew
the type well. They lived in a poor village, and seven brothers had gotten together, pooled their money, and sent these two south, looking for
wives.

Because of their own country's short-sighted "one child" policy,
girls were in short supply, most being killed at birth or aborted as soon
as the sex of the child was known. Sons who could work, and provide
for the family, were more desirable.

Within a generation, this caused a shortage of women in their own
country. Now brides in China could demand, and expect, huge "bride
prices" in exchange for marriage.

What goes around comes around and bad Karma is a bitch.

The Vietnamese "wife" would be taken to a Chinese village where
she knew no one and couldn't speak the language. There she would be
shared among all seven brothers. Since they all lived together in one
house, each night she would be the "wife" of a different brother.

Since no Chinese woman would willingly marry into such a hard,
low-class life, these men had to go abroad to find wives. The girls, once
sold, could look forward to a life time of cleaning a squalid house, the
smell of rotting fish, and being passed from brother to brother every
night.

Naturally, the younger and prettier the girl, the higher the price.
Since these men could only afford second class "merchandise," it gave
Johnny Tran an opportunity to rid himself of the undesirable women in
his employ.

Johnny Tran had a couple of girls that fit that description.

Because of a previous failure, Johnny needed to make an example
of the girls. They sat together in a room awaiting their fate. Leather dog
collars were put around their necks. Their handlers were careful to only
beat and punch them around the head, where their hair would cover
the bruising.

When the time came they were handcuffed together, right wrist to
left wrist, and led down the hallway. The girls could hear coarse laugh-

ter from the room up ahead, as they walked toward their fate. They kept their eyes down, the other girls didn't dare look at them.

After the meal, "snake wine" was served. This increased the brothers libido as the girls came to take away their plates. Once the brothers were properly fed and watered, the girls would be brought in, and a final price would be reached.

Their handler opened the door and pushed them roughly into the room, causing one of the girls to stumble. They were led naked on a leash to stand in front of the brothers.

"What is this?" One of the brothers said, "This isn't the same quality as the girls you had serving the food."

"Yes, you're right," said Johnny Tran, "If you want top quality, then you have to pay for top quality." Lo Chin remained silent in the background.

The brothers grumbled a bit and pulled the girls closer so that one girl was standing in front of each brother. They inspected each girl as one would inspect a horse. Rough calloused hands and dirty fingernails pinched and grabbed.

"Are they virgins?" One brother asked, sticking his finger into a vagina.

"Of course not," said Johnny Tran.

They grunted, and the inspection continued. The brothers each took a leash and steered the girls towards the window in order to get a better look at them in the sunlight.

One brother had them open their mouths so he could inspect their teeth. The other brother wanted one to bend over and touch her toes, so he could examine her ass.

"As you can see, neither girl has had children yet, so they are still able to bear."

The girls stared straight ahead, mechanically suffering the various indignities. They both looked out through the window. They knew their life was over. All that was left was an endless string of days of the lowest life possible. They stared out the window and could see the rooftops of various buildings over the city.

The girls looked at each other and nodded. Then both yanked their leashes from the hands of the brothers and together ran, and crashed through the window, ending their young lives on the broken bricks below.

"Effective leadership is putting first things first. Effective management is discipline, carrying it out."

Stephen Covey

Chapter 15

The two Chinese brothers looked out the window, to the broken, bleeding bodies below.

Johnny Tran didn't bother to get up. He looked at Lo Chin and shrugged his shoulders. Lo Chin had no expression at all.

When the brothers returned to the table, Johhny Tran snapped his fingers at the man guarding the door, who hurried over, bending his head so Johnny could whisper in his ear. The man hurried out to fetch two more girls.

"More snake wine?" Johnny Tran asked the two brothers.

After the brothers were satisfied and left, Lo Chin excused himself and headed downtown to another restaurant.

Soon Lo Chin was standing at the cutting table of a District One restaurant in Saigon weighing his options. Before him stood two of his lieutenants and one of his soldiers, the soldier had been caught skimming money from Lo Chin's prostitutes who worked the De Tham District.

On one hand Lo Chin didn't begrudge the boy stealing the money. He knew the soldier's pay was low, and as a soldier in his early years, he had done the same. Of course, he was smart enough not to have ever been caught. On the other, the disrespect couldn't be overlooked. Everyone present knew that. The same as the soldier knew the penalty if he was caught.

"When was the last time you had snake blood?" Lo Chin asked the soldier.

"At least three years ago,"

"It is very good for your heart, as well as circulation."

"So I am told,"

Lo Chin reached into the bag at his feet casually, grasping a cobra by the back of its neck, and pulled the long, black snake out of the bag. The snake writhed and squirmed around Lo Chin's arm. He held the snake out at arm's reach. It was about 5 feet in length. Picking up a knife from the table, he made a quick incision in the cobra's neck, squeezing the snake's organs out through the hole and depositing them in shot glasses on the table.

Lo Chin made another incision near the base of the tail, put the knife down, and starting at the neck, squeezed the blood from the snake, depositing it into the glasses on the table. He worked quickly and expertly. He laid the dead snake on the table and motioned the men towards the glasses. The snake writhed in death and muscle memory next to the glasses.

"To good health, a happy wife, and lots of sons," he toasted.

His men came forward. Each took a glass of snake blood and gonads, and downed the whole drink in one swallow. The other lieutenants stepped back, leaving the soldier in place alone in front of the table.

Lo Chin peeled the skin off the snake expertly, pulling the scaly, bloody skin off the tail. Using a Chinese cooking knife, he laid the snake on the table and chopped the snake up into small, round steaks.

"Do you like snake meat?" Lo Chin asked the soldier.

"Yes, I do."

"Do you prefer snake meat, or dog meat?"

"I prefer dog meat, if I can get it."

Using the tip of the knife blade, Lo Chin expertly flicked each snake patty up into the air, where it fell on a hibachi on the edge of the table. He could have been a table chef at Beni Hana's.

"Did I not make the rules clear in the beginning?"

"Yes, you did."

"So you are telling me then, you're just greedy."

"No, sir. My family needed more money."

"Do you have a sick mother, or child? You could have come to me. I would have given you the money."

The soldier was quiet.

Lo Chin looked up at his lieutenants, and they immediately grabbed the soldier. One took his arm, and put his hand on the cutting board, locking his wrist in place. Picking up the knife he just used to cut up the snake, Lo Chin, spread the soldier's fingers out on the board. Then the lieutenant holding his wrist grabbed the three fingers of his hand, leaving the little finger exposed and alone.

Lo Chin turned away and flipped the snake steaks over to cook on the other side.

He turned back and rested the blade of the knife on the end of the soldier's little fingernail.

"This is how it has to be, you know," he said to the soldier.

"Yes sir, I know."

"You accept this punishment, then?"

The soldier nodded his head.

"This is the first time for you, so I will go easy on you. Make no mistake if it happens again I won't be so generous. Do you understand?"

"Yes sir, I do."

Lo Chin then leaned into the blade, cutting cleanly through the tip of the soldier's little finger, severing the fingernail in half. Lo Chin looked into the soldier's eyes the whole time. He didn't make a sound. They both looked down at the tip of the finger on the cutting board. Blood flowed out of the wound, staining the butcher block table.

Lo Chin looked into the soldier's eyes. His arm and wrist were still held fast, bloody pinky extended.

"Watch,"

The soldier looked down.

Rocking the knife back and forth, Lo Chin, with the finesse of world-class chef cleanly, and quickly sliced the soldier's little finger into a half-dozen, thin, miniature steaks, just like the snake. Like he was chopping carrots, all the way up to the second knuckle.

The lieutenants released the soldier, and Lo Chin threw the soldier a rag, which he quickly wrapped around his hand.

"Help yourself to the snake meat," Lo Chin said to everyone present.

Lo Chin left the kitchen. He had to see to loading this month's consignment of girls for transport to the United States.

"The way brainwashing works is subtle and takes a long time."

Scan Durkin

Chapter 16

Lo Chin and Johnny Tran went to choose girls for the next ship-ment to the US. It wasn't long before the girls started showing up. Lots of girls. Johnny Tran picked twenty-five of the prettiest ones; the rest left disappointed.

Lo Chin and Johnny Tran had no problem procuring girls because they had an entire province under their control for expressly that pur-pose. These girls were not only indoctrinated, but thoroughly schooled in all methods of scamming Western men from a young age. They had now "graduated" and were going to the "Golden Mountain" to make their families proud and send money back home. All were willing to pay ten thousand dollars each for the 'privilege'. They would work the debt off once they reached the US.

Besides being very beautiful, Vietnamese girls have a special magic about them; a certain mystique that is not easily defined. One is the fact that outwardly, the side they show a prospective mark, is that they were raised from birth to be the perfect wife in the old-fashioned sense of the word. To this day, one of Vietnam's major "exports" is their women.

They cook, they clean; they take care of the children and all as-pects of the house. They are willing and adventurous sexual partners in private. Many hold down jobs as well and are the principal wage earn-ers. This is important because the main output and contribution of the normal Vietnamese male is drinking, screwing, and gambling.

The women exude the appearance that they live to make their men happy. They appear shy, demure, and submissive.

Nothing could be further from the truth.

They have learned to survive the hard way. Through famine, and war, Vietnamese women survived by guile and duplicity, and they are masters at it. Vietnamese men, of course, know this and treat them badly because of it. A foreigner used to Western women, is a helpless victim, and completely unprepared for the arsenal of weapons of seduction Vietnamese girls can employ in any given situation.

What few people realize, or even comprehend, is how under the control of men some of these girls are. It defies anything found in Western culture. In the provinces under the control of Lo Chin in Southern Vietnam, the girls are beaten, sexually abused from a young age, and brainwashed. They have been cultivated for generations of conditioning to serve these men. It is ingrained into their mothers, their community, their religion, and their family life.

The Vietnamese girls are taught that all their problems are caused by the West, especially the French and Americans, and that Westerners "owe" the Vietnamese. Therefore, most Vietnamese thought it was perfectly all right to lie, scam or cheat foreigners whenever possible.

Lo Chin, and by extension, Johnny Tran, had complete control over the girls via their families who were indebted to him.

The process works like this: The girls are treated as useless from birth and not shown any love from their fathers, which establishes a deep yearning for affection as well as approval from males. They are raped and sexually abused from a young age, usually with "training" starting between five and seven years old. They are sexually abused by their fathers, grandfathers, even uncles and brothers. By thirteen they are ready to enter the sex trade.

The purpose is to break their will and force them to become numb robots. The less emotion these girls feel, the better tool they are in executing these scams. Lo Chin could completely control these girls and force them to do things that they sometimes didn't want to do. They knew they would be beaten or sold as life-long sex-slaves if they didn't comply.

The girls are taught to prey on Westerners every chance they get. They are sent to schools, where Western teachers worked. They get jobs in Western businesses. They are told to marry Western husbands.

The girls are taught how to get Western men to fall in love with them so they can hack his computers, his cell phone, learn about him and patiently wait until they scam or kill him for his money. They usually blackmail the guy and the men are too scared to report it to the police due to embarrassment and fear of divorce.

Lo Chin, who operates the saunas and massage parlors, as well as restaurants in Saigon, runs his businesses like a concentration camp and will have the girls beaten, or sell them in Mongolia, Korea or Indonesia if they refuse to scam the Western guys when called upon to do so. Others simply disappeared when they did something wrong, leaving the rest of the girls who work for Johnny Tran in absolute fear for their lives.

They are hit for little or no reason. Twenty-five percent or more of the girls always wore black and blue marks from being disciplined. The managers punched them in the head where their hair would cover up the bruises. Sometimes the beatings got out of hand, and the girls had scars and visible marks on their body to prove it.

The girls are back-handed if they call off work for anything other than their menstrual cycle, and forced to have sex with up to eight guys a day if they are popular enough to be picked that many times.

If Lo Chin, or one of his lieutenants suspected a girl to be lying about her menstrual cycle, they would force her to come to work and a manager would physically put his finger in her and check that she is truly on her period.

On the monthly off days, they worked the nail salons and were hostesses at his restaurants.

The blackmail and extortion scams were usually executed against the Western men if Johnny Tran could get hidden video or information that would embarrass the victim. If they found out you have a wife and family in your home country, even better. The basic approach is always the same although the ending varies. But blackmail is always the end game.

The chosen girls were loaded into a forty foot container bound for Chicago. They lived in the container for the entire twenty day ocean crossing. When they got hungry, they had crackers, rice and water. When the seas turned rough, they had buckets for toilets. They were allowed out of the container once a day for 'entertainment' by the crew of the ship. From Chicago, the container was loaded onto the back of a semi-truck to make the final leg of the journey to Des Moines. Some of the girls wouldn't ever see Chicago, Des Moines, or the US.

Johnny Tran knew from past experience that, on average, at least five of the girls would die in transit. He considered it 'spoilage.'

"Bruce Lee only played himself."

Leo Howard

Chapter 17

Wee and Cobalt stood watching a 9th. Degree black belt doing his warming up kicks.

Cobalt decided he needed a driver/bodyguard since the carjacking to prevent future occurrences. Cobalt had never seen anyone faster with their elbows or knees, which was why he and Wee were now at a martial arts dojo downtown.

Cobalt explained to the black belt in Tai Kwon Do that he wanted to assess Wee's abilities as part of a job interview. Cobalt enlightened the Sensei that Wee was trained in Muay Thai, the Thai martial art. He paid the head teacher handsomely, and said he'd pay double it if he could take Wee down.

The black belt immediately got suited up. He had more foam padding on than the Michelin Man. He looked like the Pillsbury Dough Boy with a black belt.

Wee disdained any sort of protective gear. Not even gloves.

"I don't hit with my fists," Wee explained to Cobalt watching the instructor suit up, "You'll hurt your hands, then they are useless. Only an amateur uses his fists as an offensive weapon."

Wee, smiled idiotically and looked like Cobalt's retarded, inbred brother. He took off his shirt, folded it, then took off his shoes. He set his folded shirt on the seat of a metal chair and arranged his shoes under it.

Wee ducked under the rope, and entered the ring barefoot.

A crowd gathered around. A couple of bets were placed discreetly on how long it would take the black belt to dispatch this Asian idiot. Wee stood there and looked for all the world like he was waiting for a city bus. His hands weren't up, his feet in no discernible fighting stance.

The black belt danced to this side and that. He threw mock punches like a boxer. He made fancy kicks towards Wee's face, but stopped them before they connected. Wee never moved, never even flinched. He stood there smiling.

The black belt never landed a punch or, a kick.

The match was over in less time than it took the black belt to suit up. In fact, it looked like Wee stood still. When he did move, he moved so fast, and so deadly, it was over in the blink of an eye. The black belt was down on the mat, face up, staring incredulously into Wee's laughing eyes. Wee helped him up with good humor.

Wee looked over at Cobalt and said in Thai, "He's not understanding his opponent. You should stop this. This is not an equal match."

"My colleague said that we should end this match," Cobalt said to the black belt, "otherwise someone could get hurt."

"He said that, did he?" Answered the black belt, ego bruised, not wanting to back down in front of his school. The black belt took off his protective gear and now faced Wee in a black gee. The pace of the betting picked up. Students slapped down money openly now. Twenties were piled up along with an occasional C-note.

"There is no dishonor here," said Wee, again to Cobalt in Thai, "but he fights like a school teacher. He doesn't understand the concept of total war. Call this off Cobalt, or this on your head."

"My colleague said he doesn't want to fight. That you are the superior fighter, and he is afraid..."

At that moment the black belt attacked for real, full force, straight at Wee.

To call what happened next a slaughter would be to embarrass abattoirs everywhere. Again, Wee didn't even seem to move, and the black belt was down on the mat. Face down, and not moving. One arm was twisted behind his back. Cobalt couldn't tell if it was broken or not.

Cobalt was paying attention this time. He filmed it with his cell phone and was able to play it back later in slow motion. As soon as the black belt attacked, Wee was up in the air and had hit the black belt four times, once with each knee to the kidney, and once with the striking end of each elbow. The last elbow strike was to the back of the neck as he was already going down, driving the black belt face down onto the mat. It happened in the split second it took for Wee to fall back to the floor, exactly where he started.

"Jesus Christ, Wee…" Cobalt muttered under his breath, "Did you have to do that?"

Wee shrugged his shoulders. "It was the force of his attack. I had no choice. His own momentum did that to him."

Wee was still standing in the same position, looking for all the world like he was still waiting for the number six bus to come. Wee's mask slipped off for a fraction of a second, then it was replaced just as quickly with his patented idiotic smile. Wee checked the pulse on the black belt's neck, made an "Oh well, he was warned" gesture with his hands and climbed out of the ring.

Cobalt called an ambulance on his cell phone and made arrangements to pay the medical bill.

Wee put his shoes and shirt back on then walked over to the gamblers. Still smiling idiotically, not saying a word, he held out his hand, palm up, in a "I'll take my share now" gesture.

They gave Wee the entire amount collected.

The first principle of contract negotiations is don't remind them of what you did in the past - tell them what you're going to do in the future.

Stan Musial

Chapter 18

While Wee may have had the bodyguard part of his job description down pat, the 'driver' part left a lot of be desired.

Thais drive on the left-hand side of the road, opposite the US, which completely screwed-up Wee's sense of direction. The second problem getting in the way of smooth driving was Wee had never driven a standard transmission. Cobalt himself tried at first tried to instruct Wee in the finer arts of a seven-speed. After fifteen minutes of Cobalt fearing for life and limb, he decided a professional was better suited for the job.

At first, Cobalt had no problem with Wee using his Porsche to practice in. After listening to the gears grind, the sudden stops, jolts, and tire squeals, he decided it might be better if Wee learned on an automatic transmission.

He needed Wee to learn defensive, as well as offensive driving. But not turning from the left hand lane across all traffic to make a right-hand turn was going to have to come first.

He left Wee in the hands of the driving instructor and went car shopping with Ning.

One month later, Wee pulled smoothly to the curb in a black BMW 750i sedan. It was a beauty. It was customized exactly the way Cobalt wanted it and delivered on time. Flat-proof tires, bullet-proof glass, re-inforced bumpers if ramming ever became an issue and enough weapons hidden under the trunk to defend a small nation.

Wee jumped out of the driver's side in full expectation of opening the back door for his boss, the way he'd seen in the movies. He was wondering if he should ask Cobalt about getting a chauffeur's uniform. Ning could get in on the other side in the traffic.

Ning quickly stepped in front of Cobalt, handed Wee a dollar as a tip, and got in first. Cobalt got in last, with Wee standing at the door, fuming at the insult.

As soon as they got into the car, Ning rolled up the privacy glass, cutting Wee off in mid sentence.

Wee rolled it back down.

"Where to, Boss?" he asked.

"Once around the park, driver," said Ning, and rolled the privacy glass back up.

Cobalt hit the interior intercom, "Wee? Let's go to the in-town apartment."

Wee rolled the privacy glass back down. "Okay, Boss!"

Cobalt's in town apartment was done in Asian antique. It is a man's apartment with books on business, war, philosophy, and lots of weapons. Cobalt collected antique weapons from past battles which were displayed on the walls. One of Jean Lafitte's deck cannons from the Battle of New Orleans, sat on the floor in the corner. Muskets from the Civil War were also on display. He kept his personal armory here, locked in another room. In his armory he had sniper rifles, and advanced military weapons. He also had the latest in any business electronics here as well. The apartment was swept weekly for bugs by a private security firm.

The apartment was located in the business district. It was kept extremely neat by a maid that came in three times a week. Cobalt preferred to do any personal business here, rather than invite anyone back to his house. It was an iron-clad rule he had observed for ten years... until Ning and Wee came calling anyway.

Wee plopped down on the sofa and started channel surfing for the Cartoon Network. The kitchen wasn't as extensive, or as comfortable here, so Ning just slid up to the breakfast counter, and kicked off her shoes.

"Good job today, Ning," said Cobalt, meaning it. "That was a tough negotiation. You handled it with ease."

"It was easy. They sincerely wanted to believe their own bullshit. I just made it acceptable for them to do so."

"Still, it was an excellent piece of work...," said Cobalt, remembering...

Ning and Cobalt walked into the conference room at precisely nine AM. The room was already occupied by two CEO's and no less than nine lawyers, all sitting in tandem on the other side of the table. A few of the gentlemen stood when Ning entered; most did not. No one offered to shake hands or introduce themselves. It looked like little ol Ning and Cobalt against an army.

Two against eleven.

If it had been thirty, thought Cobalt, it might have been a fair fight.

"Let's get to it," said one of the CEO's, glaring at Cobalt. "One hundred and fifty million. Take or leave it."

"We'll leave it," said Ning rising. Cobalt rose with her. "Thank you gentlemen for wasting our time. My consolation is this private army of lawyers today must have cost a fortune."

"Come on, Jack, no reason to be hostile to the pretty lady," said the lead attorney smoothly, "We all want the same thing."

"What would that be?" Asked Ning.

"An equitable deal, of course. We're all professionals here."

"And one hundred and fifty million is your idea of an equitable deal?"

"It is."

"I was thinking more along the lines of sixty-five million," said Ning, looking straight at the second CEO, smiling coyly.

He was younger, and considered himself a lady's man. Ning had done her homework and knew, out of the entire battalion present, he was the only one that mattered. She had psychological profiles and background investigations done on everyone present. Cobalt, for his part, remained silent and watched the other players.

This is going to be interesting, he thought.

Ning, who became his VP of negotiations, immediately took to the subtleties of her position with ease. She was also a tiger in the boardroom. She could completely disarm opponents with her beauty, then when the time was right, make them agree to terms that were clearly not in their best interest over the objections of their own counsel. The opposing team would leave the negotiations smiling like they had gotten the better part of the deal. Cobalt had never seen anything like it. So he made her his chief negotiator at once.

Cobalt knew when he was out-matched, and when to delegate.

"I wouldn't even let you park my car for that much," said the CEO, but he was falling under Ning's spell. Cobalt could see it.

"It's not your car I want to park," said Ning. "Let's try looking at this from another point of view, shall we?" Ning got up and walked to the front of the table. All eyes were on her, especially the younger CEO. Cobalt could swear he saw him lick his lips.

"Now, imagine this…" Between the subtle fragrance of her perfume, and her expensive outfit, which accentuated all the right curves, every single man in the room was imagining something, but it wasn't the deal. Ning wove a spell. She hypnotized them with her movements, and her beauty. Soon heads were nodding in assent. She wrapped up the presentation by leaning on the conference table, giving them all a quick peep into her cleavage.

"You can clearly see, at sixty-five million, you have a more advantageous offer on the table than even one hundred and fifty million."

"Well, I see your point, but I think even at that rate of return, one hundred million is more than fair," said the CEO, but he was buckling. One of the lawyers leaned over, whispered in his ear, nodding his head.

"Seventy-five million, but we keep the stock options and Internet properties."

The deal was finalized, and Cobalt and Ning walked out of the conference room.

Cobalt shook himself out of the memory.

"You know that company is worth two hundred million, don't you?"

"Of course, I do. When they said one hundred and fifty million, I knew I had them and they had undervalued."

"Well, you earned Wee's and your Christmas bonus, this year."

Wee stuck his head over the couch at the mention of his name.

"Yes, she sure did," Wee said in Thai, "Hey Ning, here's a Christmas bonus from me…"

He farted.

"The thousands of criminals I have seen in 40 years of law enforcement have had one thing in common: Every single one was a liar."

J. Edgar Hoover

Chapter 19

Vietnamese criminals all approach you with a smile.

It's not like the movies where there is a cocky Asian Guy with tattoos acting tough, as he scrapes his Samurai sword across the asphalt, sparks flying.

Vietnamese criminals dress nicely, come off as legitimate businessmen and also run legitimate businesses. They are polite, soft spoken and smile often in a self-depreciating way. In a land of huge business egos, like the USA, they are almost always underestimated. But the crimes they are plotting and committing behind the scenes are more evil than anything you see in the movies.

They not only steal everything you have, they want to take your heart and soul too.

They also like to keep their operations confined to the Vietnamese community. Rarely do their criminal activities involve outsiders. This is a community which history has taught to distrust law enforcement or any government official. A community which is well versed in keeping their mouth's shut.

They brought all the bad habits of the old country to the US when Saigon fell in 1975. The criminal element came with them and was flourishing within minutes of arrival on American shores.

They started out with nail salons and single-handedly created much of the beauty culture in America, cornering the entire US market from coast to coast with fast, cheap, nails. So much so, that today Americans would have a hard time entering it. Together with the Vietnamese penchant for frugality and cutting corners on quality, soon laws and licensing had to be enacted to reign in the most abusive practices. Not to be deterred, the Vietnamese bought, or built, the nail schools for which licensing depended. They set up their own diploma mills, and financed more nail salons.

Since Vietnamese women are known the world over for their beauty, and since nail service always employs massage, massage parlors and prostitution were a natural second income stream. Where you have prostitution, drugs are never far away.

As Vietnamese cuisine became more popular, the Vietnamese mafia was there with the front money for anyone interested in opening a restaurant. In addition, it gave them a way to put their women to work in more traditional fashion, when they got too old for prostitution.

They even settled, and built their own cities. Westminster, or "Little Saigon" in California, being the biggest. They had their own TV stations, radio stations and newspapers. Like most Asians, they settled around other Vietnamese. Every city in America now has a neighborhood that is called "Little Vietnam."

While the black and Hispanic gangs, and occasionally the Chinese Triads got all the negative press, the Vietnamese could stay under the radar of law enforcement. What the world saw was quiet, hard-working, immigrants. For the most part, they were. A small minority of the criminal element controlled the money and business. Because of their distrust of police and government, the Vietnamese policed themselves.

Johnny Tran was the Chief of the Vietnamese Police in Des Moines, Iowa.

Johnny Tran plans rarely failed due to his absolute patience and attention to detail.

Tran's business and criminal strategy was as simple as it was brutal. He explained it to one of his soldiers this way,

"What you cannot steal, you buy.

"If you can't buy it, then try a bribe.

"If they cannot be bribed, then you blackmail, if they have any vices.

"If they cannot be black mailed, you kidnap a family member."

"What if they do not have a family member?"

"Then you kidnap them," Johnny Tran said.

"You can't assume any place you go is private because the means of surveillance are becoming so affordable and so invisible."

Howard Rheingold

Chapter 20

Acting on a tip from Lamar, Flynn set up surveillance in time to see the girls being unloaded from the tractor trailer.

He had met Lamar twelve hours earlier.

"Yo, Flynn! You get anywhere on my problem?"

"Did you get anywhere on mine?"

"Your boy in Western Iowa still has four days on the clock. You have until then." Lamar said. "But just in case you don't come through, we're letting the string play out."

They were sitting in a coffee shop/bakery on University Avenue in West Des Moines. The kind that sold "Artisan" bread, and had about fifteen different kinds of coffee to choose from, which always confused Flynn. The college girl behind the counter looked at him like he was an idiot when he asked if they had any Maxwell House. Flynn wasn't going on a date to the prom with her.

"What's the story with Sammy Samurai?" Flynn asked.

"His name is Johnny Tran. He's a lieutenant and an enforcer in the local Vietnamese triad. He runs the Des Moines branch of the operation. He's a little boss in terms of the national hierarchy but extremely bad news. Word is, he's good with a knife. We've heard rumors that bodies are never found because they are ground up and mixed with beef at the Vietnamese restaurants."

"You believe it?" Flynn asked, wiping a chocolate croissant off his face.

"You tell me. When you were on the force, were any bodies ever laid against the Vietnamese?"

"Never."

"Exactly my point. I know for a fact they dropping them. How they able to Jimmy Hoffa all those bodies?"

"Like I said, all what bodies? The Asians like to talk big and act big. But that doesn't mean people are being ground up and served in egg rolls."

"Then I got someone you might want to talk to."

"Yeah, who?"

"One of the girls who works at a nail salon. She wants to jump ship and come work for the guys with the white hats."

"Oh, is that how you characterize yourself now, Lamar? A fine, up-standing citizen and a member of the White Hat Club. You could wear a mask over your eyes, and 'Aaron' could be your ghetto Tonto. Or just get a bat light, like Batman, and shine it over the city whenever a citizen needs help?"

"Just come and see what she has to say," Lamar said, smiling in spite of himself at Flynn's description.

Two hours later, Tram Ngoc, the Vietnamese nail tech, who did Ning's nails, entered nervously into the Allied Consultants building on the South side. Lamar came in behind her. None of the kids in the sur-rounding rooms paid the slightest bit of attention to them. Lamar led them to an office in the back.

"Go ahead, tell him." Lamar said to the girl, after they were seated.

She looked about twenty-five, although it was hard to tell, dark haired, dark eyed and pretty. Her hair was long, straight, and black. Her English was passable, obviously learned as a second language, accented, and she sometimes struggled for the correct words.

"Johnny Tran, bad man," she whispered, as though he might hear her.

"Have you ever seen him kill someone?"

"Yes. Many time. He sometime make us girls watch."

"Who does he kill?" Asked Flynn.

"The girls. You lazy, he kill you. You mouth off, he kill you. You no want fuck-fuck with customer, he kill you," she said matter of factly.

"That must get kind of expensive for him, doesn't it? I mean, his business is girls. Hard to make money from a dead girl."

"Oh no. You no understand. He have lots of girls. He have girls come in from Vietnam every month. He have girls come in tonight."

"How does he kill the girls?"

"He kill them with sword or knife. He chop off hands and feet first. At end, he chop off head."

"Why not just kill them? Why go to all the trouble?"

"Because no hand, no feet, no head, girls cannot be identified. Also as punishment because now she can't get into Vietnamese heaven."

"What does he do with the bodies afterwards?"

"I no see. But boys in nail salon say they are chopped up. Meat go to restaurant, bones go to grinder."

Flynn sat back in his chair, looking at the girl.

Is it possible? He thought to himself. *Could they actually be disposing of bodies in this fashion with no one the wiser? If it is true, this girl is extraordinarily brave talking to him.*

"You say more girls are coming in tonight?"

"Yes."

"How does he bring them in?"

"Produce truck come from Chicago. They unload girls then, at back of restaurant."

Which was how Flynn came to be sitting in his cab watching the back of the Dac Biet restaurant. He couldn't see much at that distance, but it didn't make much difference. He mounted a wireless low-light camera at both entrances of the alley. He could watch the whole thing on his computer screen, out of the range of suspicion.

The truck backed down the alley carefully, using hand signals from someone on the ground. He signed the truck to stop with the universal clasped fist signal, then banged on the back of the truck.

Then Johnny Tran showed up to oversee the operation. He was easy to pick out because of the sword on his back. First, the produce was off loaded quickly and efficiently by a gang of Asian workers there for that purpose. Flynn watched as Johnny Tran paid them off in cash when they were finished. They quickly dispersed.

Other preparations were then made. Flynn couldn't see what was going on as it happened inside the restaurant. Then, on cue, one by one, the girls started coming out of the back of the truck. Some were unsteady walking. Others were getting off the truck and vomiting.

Another player walked up the alley, his back to the camera. He was dressed in a suit and didn't belong with the other riff-raff. He also looked tall for an Asian. He talked to Tran for a while. Then Tran pulled one girl out of the line. The girl kept her head down, but her body looked under aged. Tran held her by the upper arm as he talked to the newcomer, then pushed the girl towards him. The girl balked, and shook her head back and forth in a 'no' gesture. The newcomer backhanded her, and then drug her off the way he came.

After he left, another woman came up to Johnny Tran and started talking to him. This one was older. Johnny twice made a "get in there" gesture to the woman, pointing with his thumb towards the door. The woman kept on arguing.

The third time, the sword came out in flash, and the next moment, Flynn could see the woman's head come off her shoulders and roll under the truck. Johnny Tran fished it out with the point of his sword, then kicked the head towards one of his workers to dispose of. Two other workers dragged the corpse quickly inside.

Flynn counted twenty-one girls.

Flynn tapped a few keys on his keyboard, saved the video in an encrypted file, and picked up his cell phone. He searched an unlisted cell phone directory, found the number he was looking for, and pressed the green "call" button.

He called Ning.

The phone rang then, and Ning picked it up.

"Cobalt Industries."

"You dress them up; you send them to school. Still they don't write, they don't call. Kids, these days…"

Ning recognized Flynn's voice immediately.

"I was wondering if you'd be bright enough to track me down."

Banter between the kids stopped in a heartbeat. Ning was staring straight at Cobalt. Wee clicked the cartoon network off. Flynn picked up on the sudden background silence.

"I hope I'm not interrupting anything."

"As a matter fact you are. Get to the point."

"Let's just say, I'm going to need your help soon."

"Why would I help a taxi driver? You must have me confused with your dispatcher."

"Because of my winning smile and witty repartee…because you lust for another chance to see me…"

"Does this have anything to do with that idiot we saw in the nail salon?"

"…And because I know you want to help your countrymen."

"I'm Thai. Not Vietnamese. Besides, they do shitty nails."

"Vinny's Cafe. Right down the street from your boss's pad. You know, where you are right now."

"When?"

"How about an hour? I'm on a tight timetable."

"How do I know I can trust you?" Ning asked.

"You don't," Then the line was dead.

" Good things happen when you meet strangers."

Yo-Yo Ma

Chapter 21

"You want to explain what that phone call was about? You been cheating on me?" Cobalt said smiling, looking at Ning.

Their relationship wasn't sexual and it never would be, much to Cobalt's, and Ning's, secret dismay.

"I'd never cheat on you Max, you know that. Screw around on the side maybe, but never cheat."

Wee, who knew Ning better than Cobalt, eyed her with interest.

"What did you get yourself involved in?" Wee said, after a long pause.

"I'm not sure."

"OK, then. What just happened?"

"I met this cab driver the other day…"

Flynn sat in Vinny's Cafe waiting for Ning to show up. He was slightly amused when he saw her show up with two men in tow, in a classic bodyguard sandwich, one in front, one in back.

He didn't recognize the one in front, a wiry Asian guy, hands at his sides, walking on the balls of his feet. Flynn knew the look. Even though Flynn outweighed him by seventy-five pounds, he knew he would be a formidable opponent.

It was the guy bringing up the rear that took his breath away.

Flynn felt the familiar feeling in the pit of his stomach that signaled the arriving of his mentor and ghost. This time however, it was a powerful rush of heat that radiated out to every part of his body. The man in the rear was a dead ringer for Flynn's ghost…except thirty years younger.

This must be Max Cobalt.

Flynn's ghost sat down next to him and decided to giggle.

Great.

Ning sat opposite Flynn in the booth. Max Cobalt sat next to Ning. The Asian guy moved in next to Flynn and clamped one of Flynn's hands under the table, while the other hand expertly frisked him.

"You always come with an entourage?" Flynn asked Ning evenly.

Wee found Flynn's 9mm in his shoulder holster and palmed it under the table to Cobalt. Flynn heard the safety go off and knew the gun was pointed at his balls.

"You missed the one in my ankle holster," Flynn said to Wee.

"Try reaching for it and see if you can get to it in time," said Wee.

Flynn looked at Cobalt then. Expressionless blue eyes stared back at him. Flynn could read nothing. Flynn felt an unexpected warm rush of feeling towards him. Cobalt felt it too. There was confusion in his eyes for a second, then his eyes turned blank again.

"Do we know each other?" Cobalt asked.

"No sir, we don't."

Ning decided it was time to jump into the conversation.

"First thing. I don't know your name."

"Everybody calls me Flynn."

"Is that your first name or last name?" Ning asked, playing on their conversation in the cab.

"Both." Flynn replied, picking up on the double entendre.

"Do you always track the people down you pick up in your cab, Flynn?"

"Nope. I'm not a cab driver."

"Right. You just drive a cab for fun."

"Sometimes."

"What do you do?"

"I solve problems," Flynn said, smiling at Cobalt wondering if he knew he had a step-mother and sister. Cobalt, for his part, had the uneasy feeling this guy knew more about him than he allowed people to know. Flynn's smile said he knew secrets.

"And I have a problem you want to solve…?" Ning asked.

"No, I have a problem I want you to help *me* solve."

"And what problem do you have that you want me to help *you* solve?"

Flynn pulled his eyes away from Cobalt and looked at Ning.

"I want you to become a call girl," Flynn said, then burst out laughing. "Don't worry, I pay well."

"For Christ's sake. Let's get out of here," Ning said to the table, rolling her eyes.

"I can also use your boyfriend here," Flynn nodded in Wee's direction, "He looks like a degenerate gambler."

Cobalt's left hand shot up like a schoolboy having to go pee, the one not holding the 9mm.

"Can I be a flaming gay and wear a tutu?"

"If it gives you morning wood, I won't object," Flynn said, deadpan.

*Careful, he's not someone you want to fuck with...*said the small internal voice of his ghost.

"Oh, doesn't this look like a happy crowd," said a waitress, coming to the table. What can I getcha?"

"We'll have coffees all around."

"You guys want menus?"

"Nah, just coffee for now, and some privacy."

"Don't get touchy. I'll have your coffees in a jiffy."

The table was silent as the waitress got the coffee, mugs, and condiments. She poured coffee from her hip as she set the cups down.

"Can I get you anything else?"

"That's going to do it. Thanks."

The waitress walked away, job done, and moved on to other customers uninterested in the table behind her.

"OK, here's the deal," Flynn began, after the waitress left, "That nail salon I picked you up at the other day has some things going on that my client wants to see stopped."

"Who's your client?" Ning asked.

Flynn looked at Ning in silence.

Stupid question, his look said.

"Here's what I can tell you. These are bad guys. The job is dangerous. You won't be doing anything illegal, just playacting, but it can get you hurt all the same. I want you to go to a card game."

"I'm in," Wee said quickly, anything for a chance to gamble on someone else's dime. "Can I play five-card stud? What are the stakes?"

"Oh yeah. I can pretty much guarantee it. No limit. If it goes down the way I hope, and the way I've planned, you'll be removing some human trafficking scum and freeing some girls."

"Ohhh…Caped Crusader and cab driver, uh?" Ning said, sarcastically.

"Do your plans always go down the way you hope and plan?" asked Cobalt.

"Almost never," answered Flynn, honestly. "Do yours?"

"My odds are about the same," Cobalt conceded. "What's the set up?"

"Your boyfriend here…" indicating Wee, "…What's your name, anyway?"

"Wee."

"Wee here will go in as a gambler to a high stakes game. Ning, you'll be his eye-candy. Illegal card games sometimes get ripped off. Like what will happen the night you're there. You don't have to do anything. Just act scared shitless along with everybody else. One guy is going to make a stand. You'll know who it is. He'll probably get hurt. After the robbery, just get the fuck out like everyone else. That's it."

"What about the cops?"

"I'll take care of the cops."

"So why do you need us?"

"I need someone on the inside to feed me details. You'll be wired. The timing has to be perfect."

"I guess you forgot that little detail. What if they find the wire?"

"Then you're fucked."

"And you get to keep the pot along with taking out your business rival, is that it?" asked Cobalt.

"I'm not in it for the money. You can keep it if you want. And he's not my business rival."

"What are you in it for?"

Flynn dropped his eyes and stared at his fingernails. "I just want to make the world a better place, and solve someone else's problem," he said, sincerely.

Anyone else saying that line and Cobalt would have laughed in their face. In Flynn, he saw a deep-seated sorrow, and a man yearning to make amends for past wrongs.

Flynn wanted redemption, and back in the human race, more than anything else.

Flynn heard the safety to the 9mm engage, a rustle under the table as Cobalt passed the weapon back to Wee under the table, then Wee slid it back into Flynn's shoulder holster as quickly as a pick-pocket.

"Where am I going to be when all this is going down," asked Cobalt.

"At home knitting your tutu for all I care."

"My people, my responsibility. They only move after I've checked you out, and I give the final okay."

Flynn looked up then and straight into Cobalt's eyes.

"You any relation to that guy who got killed four years ago in that Jeffery Prescott mess?"

"No." The answer was flat. The tone said, 'don't go there.'

"Wanna bet?" Flynn said, quietly.

Flynn felt his ghost smile.

"I took a psychology class, and I think the study of the mind can help me further my acting ability. It's also taught me about getting into an environment with new people and acting like you've known them forever."

Sierra McCormick

Chapter 22

Flynn and Cobalt sat down the street in the yellow cab, listening as Ning and Wee got ready to make their entrance. It was decided Ning should wear the wire since there was less chance of her being searched, or the wire found.

Ning and Wee didn't have a formal invite, but both being Asian, they figured they could fake it.

"One, two, shake a shoe…," Ning said, testing her mike.

"Three, four, grab a whore…" Wee chimed in for good measure, nuzzling her cleavage.

Flynn tapped the horn quickly letting them know he could hear them fine.

Ning pushed him away. "Pervert."

"Soi Cowboy whore…" Wee retorted. "Remember, you're my eye-candy. No mouthing off."

"Then no groping."

"I have to grope. It's my job to grope!"

"You touch me below the waist and I'll break your hand. Fuck Flynn. He can save mankind without you groping my privates."

"To snip, or not to snip, tis the question…" Wee said, paraphrasing Shakespeare. "Tis better to suffer the slings and arrows…by the way, Ning, you never told me. Do you have a sling, or an arrow?"

Which earned Wee a crippling elbow to the solar Plexus before climbing the stairs to the card game.

"What they hell are they talking about?" Flynn asked, bewildered.

"It's a crude reference to Ning's transgendered status."

"Ning is a he? Are you shitting me?"

"Truthfully, I don't know. She's never told any of us if she went in for the surgery."

"That isn't possible. That's all woman." A pause, then... "Are you tapping that?"

"Fuck no."

"Why not?"

"Because she's the best negotiator and strategic thinker I've ever had. A personal relationship would fuck up my company. I can't risk it."

"So then, you don't mind if I..."

"Oh that, I would love to see." Cobalt burst out laughing. "Maybe I should knit a tutu for you, too, Flynn."

The banter was replaced with the noise of two people walking up stairs. They reached a landing, then knocked on a door. A door plate slid back.

"Invitation?"

Wee pulled out a wad of cash. "Will this do?"

"No." The door plate crashed back.

"I don't think they like you, honey." This came from Ning.

"Ya think?"

Wee pondered his next move when the door opened and Johnny Tran stood there. One hand was inside his suit coat grasping the hilt of his tanto.

"Vietnamese only. You aren't Vietnamese, this is a private party," he said, looking at their facial features.

"The nationality of my money is the only thing that matters, and it is international." Wee said, fanning about ten thousand in one hundred-dollar bills.

Johnny Tran was more interested in Ning than Wee, or his money.

Ning was pulling on Wee's arm in a silent gesture of 'let's leave.'

Wee pulled her back and cupped one of Ning's breasts. "You like that? I'll put her on the table as an ante."

"You'll need more than that."

"I have more than that."

Tran's hand eased off the knife. "The rules are simple. Any game, no limit. Pay off any debts by the end of the night. If you don't, you die.

Any trouble, you die."

"Agreed."

"Good. You're early and most of the players haven't arrived yet. We are passing the time playing strip poker with the whores."

Johnny Tran stepped aside and Wee goosed Ning in the ass causing her to jump, as they both entered the game.

Wee and Ning entered the game room. Wee had seen a thousand like it in Thailand. Here everything was for sale, trade, or barter. Especially the women. Of which they outnumbered the men three to one. All of them young and beautiful, most under-aged. Some were attached to players, others, topless, made the rounds, refilling drinks. Any of the unattached females could be used by the players if they wanted to sit a hand out, or just felt the need.

Cigarette smoke filled the air, hovering just under the ceiling like yellow-gray thunder clouds. On a side table, in a candy dish, was a pile of blue pills…Viagra. The table also contained many other drugs. Ecstasy, uppers, downers, and cocaine were just some of the pleasures presented. Next to the 'candy' table, was a buffet set out with various Vietnamese specialty dishes.

There were three other doors, each had an armed thug standing in front of it in a two thousand dollar suit, feet spread, hands in front, crossed over the crotch, eyes looking at nothing.

Ning had a big problem, and she knew it.

She was wearing one of her best slutty dresses and Jimmy Choo "fuck-me" shoes. Her dress was snow white, a low backless and strapless number held up by her breasts. The dress contrasted her mocha colored skin and jet-black hair perfectly. Tucked into the fabric was the wireless microphone. To make matters even more 'delicate', Ning wasn't wearing a bra, or panties. If she had to play strip poker, she had only one article of clothing, and it was coming off with the ante.

Taking off her dress meant revealing the microphone.

Revealing the microphone meant a quick, or not so quick, death.

Wee was secretly chortling to himself as well at Ning's predicament. Maybe the great debate would finally be put to rest…Did Ning go in for a sex-change operation, or not? Wee had known Ning for over fifteen years and even he didn't know the answer to that question. It would really suck if he had to die to find out.

Wee stood off to the side, surveying the room, his hand playing over Ning's ass, with Ning occasionally slapping his hand away. Johnny Tran was in back of them, watching them both closely. Ning could almost feel him licking his lips in anticipation of seeing her naked.

Wee looked around the room, choosing a game table. He was aware of Ning's problem, but it was too late to back out now. Black Jack or Stud Poker? Wee chose the five-card stud table.

Flynn had guessed correctly, Wee thought ruefully. *The plan went to shit almost from the very beginning.*

"Ante up!" Johnny Tran said in Vietnamese to the room at large.

"In preparing for battle I have always found that plans are useless,
but planning is indispensable."

Dwight D. Eisenhower

Chapter 23

"Tell me about the room, Wee!" Flynn said, to no one in particular.

Wee knew his job and without even hearing, knew what was expected of him. So did Ning.

Ning made a show of spinning around the room.

"Honey, Which of those three doors is the bathroom?"

"Well, those three, on the North, East, and West, have men standing in front of them. I don't think it's one of them. Maybe that unmarked door over there."

Johnny Tran sauntered over. "Is there a problem?"

"I'm just trying to figure out where the bathroom is. Too much champagne."

Johnny Tran gestured towards the unguarded door.

"Thanks, I'll just be a minute."

Wee looked at Johnny Tran and shrugged his shoulders. "Women and their bladders. What can I say?"

Johnny Tran admired her ass as she walked away.

Flynn picked up his cell phone, pressed some numerals, and got an answer right away.

"Four doors. Front entrance is reinforced. North, East, and West doors are guarded. Two windows facing front, one facing back. Handguns. No automatic weapons visible. Four guards, including the target."

Flynn listened for a beat, then said. "Copy," folding up his phone.

"Five minutes to kickoff." Flynn said to Cobalt.

Ning came back inside three minutes and stood beside Wee.

"Picked your game yet?" Johnny Tran said to Wee.

"I'll go with five-card stud."

"Take your place, then. The game is about to begin."

Wee looked around at the four players. Two were middle-aged men. The other was about thirty-five. Each had a girl standing to the side. None of the girls were over sixteen, except Ning. They were looking down at the floor self consciously.

"Ante up," the dealer said.

Without being told, two of the girls reached up their dresses and pulled their panties down and put them on the table. The other pulled her bra off under her dress and added it to the pile. All eyes went to Ning. She shrugged, stood on one leg, with her hand on Wee's shoulder, and pulled off one shoe and tossed it on the table.

"Unacceptable ante," one of the players said. "All the other girls added underwear."

"Why is it unacceptable?" asked Wee. "My girl isn't wearing a bra or panties. She can't add them to the pot." To stress his point, Wee pulled down Ning's top, exposing her breasts.

"See? No bra."

All eyes were on Ning's perfect tits, when the shit hit the fan.

Wee had assumed the doors would blow inward, taking out the guards. He had steeled his mind for pyrotechnics in order to not be taken by surprise.

What happened next was almost anticlimactic.

There was a tinkle of glass, then the three guards dropped to the floor simultaneously, with bullet holes in their foreheads. Hardly anyone even noticed.

For an extended second, no one knew quite what had happened. Most of the clientele were still staring at Ning's tits, oblivious to the fact that their world had just changed for the worse.

Johnny Tran wasn't fooled though. The knife came out of its sheath lightning fast, and he did a double roll away from the windows and behind the table in back of Ning and Wee.

The girls started to scream, first one, and then the other two in unison.

Johnny Tran grabbed Wee, and pulled him over backwards still in his chair, intending to use him as a human shield.

At that second, the windows blew in, and it looked like a SWAT team was raiding the place and rappelling in through the windows.

There were three of them, one through each window in perfect unison.

All the players and girls now were down on the floor with two of the commandos covering them.

One of the commandos, a wiry, black guy, with a balaclava covering his face stood alone, carrying a pump shotgun, stared at Wee and Johnny Tran.

Johnny Tran stood behind Wee and held the Japanese knife to Wee's throat.

"You honestly believe killing him is going to stop me?" Lamar said, speaking for the first time.

"Do you honestly believe I care?"

"We both know how this is going to end,"

"I do? How's it going to end?"

"From the looks of the current situation, badly."

"Badly, for you, Lamar. You should have kept your mouth shut."

Johnny Tran spun Wee around, dragging the tanto across his neck, and cutting his throat. His aim was off, dragging the razor edge across this collarbone and shoulder instead. Blood gushed from the wound, and he spun Wee and pushed him straight at Lamar, just as Lamar's shotgun went off, peppering Wee's backside and thighs with buckshot.

Johnny Tran did a straight roll and, came up swinging at Lamar. Lamar shucked his shotgun once and let loose right where he had been standing. Johnny Tran continued his roll and went straight out the window Lamar came in, head first.

Jet Li couldn't have executed that move any quicker. It was a two story drop.

Ning pulled her dress up and went to Wee's aid.

There was blood everywhere. Ning looked down at Wee and didn't think he was going to make it.

Lamar, surveyed the damage, then looked down from the window, positive Johnny Tran didn't make it.

Except Johnny Tran was nowhere in sight.

"Sometimes by losing a battle you find a new way to win the war."

Donald Trump

Chapter 24

Flynn and Cobalt were already in motion as soon as they heard the shotgun blasts. Flynn prepared some paramedics and had them standing by…just in case.

'Just in case' came in a hurry and the paramedics rolled up in front of the building in seconds. Cobalt and Flynn were jogging towards the scene when they arrived. Flynn carried a battering ram and took the reinforced front door down with two swings at the hinges. He stood aside as the flood of Asian humanity gushed out through the broken door.

When the human tide ebbed, the paramedics went in.

They first stopped the bleeding on Wee's neck by using what looked like a maxi-pad for a bandage, and wrapped it tight around the wound. It was soaked in seconds.

They rolled him over and looked at his back and thighs. His pants were shredded, but no internal organs were hit, and the femoral artery running up his leg was still intact. They put him on a stretcher and jogged their way downstairs to the ambulance.

Ning followed them downstairs with Cobalt, she wanted to go with them, herself looking like a bloody banshee. Cobalt climbed into the back of the ambulance, and Ning tried to follow. A paramedic put his hand out intending to bar her way, and instead found himself on the pavement looking up with a bare foot crushing his larynx.

"Ning? Wee thinks a paramedic might come in handy right about now," Cobalt said.

Ning, realizing the wisdom of what Cobalt was saying, helped the paramedic up. He didn't try to keep her out of the ambulance though.

The driver hit the siren and minutes later, Wee was at the hospital being rushed into surgery.

Flynn walked over to the window by Lamar, and both men stood looking down.

"How can someone get past two shotgun blasts, dive head first out of a two-story window, and walk away?" Lamar said, awe in his voice.

"It looks like one of those blasts ended up in Wee's ass."

"Collateral damage."

"Still, I'm going to have to pick up the medical bill and it would be nice if you reimbursed me."

"Consider it done."

Silence as both looked up and down the street.

"All in all, it was a good plan, Flynn. You haven't lost your touch."

"You didn't tell me it was going to be a hit."

"What did you think I was going to do? Play patty-cake?"

"Still, you can't be involving me in this shit."

They both heard the siren at the same time. It was a long way off, but the cavalry were coming. Late, and in time to clean up the mess, as usual.

"Why not?"

"Bad Karma."

"Okay, Flynn, You did your part. We be even."

"What do you mean 'even'? I was never in your debt."

"Yes, you were. One hundred large, remember?"

"I was to do a surveil and plan, which I did. You fucked the monkey on the last part, not me."

"I said, we be even. No one throwing any blame in your direction. Consider the hundred large forgiven."

In Lamar's mind, Flynn 'owed' him one hundred thousand dollars, since he lost that much. In Flynn's mind, he owed Lamar nothing, and never did. A favor for a favor. Flynn knew the argument was futile.

"Okay, time for me to split. You better too."

"Yeah."

Flynn turned away and walked a couple of steps.

"Hey, Flynn…"

"Yeah?"

Lamar just looked at him and nodded his head in respect. He brought out two cigars. Lamar lit one, and stuck the other one in

Flynn's shirt pocket.

"Later, gator."

Flynn accepted and returned the nod.

"In a while, crocodile."

Flynn sat in his office on East Walnut St. He took Lamar's cigar out of his pocket and stuck it in the pencil caddy, not knowing what else to do with it.

Thurmond Thompson walked in carrying a new briefcase moments later.

"Is it over?"

"Yeah, it's over," Flynn said.

"What's going to happen to Aaron?"

"Thurmond, there never was an 'Aaron.' Aaron is a figment of your imagination, and fevered sex dreams."

"What do you mean? I got to know him, we had a connection."

"I met Aaron. He was a black ghetto kid with gang colors and tribal tats."

"How is that possible? I saw his picture."

Flynn realized Thurmond would forever be a mark. He was incapable of learning from his mistakes. No matter how many times he got burned. If there was ever a man looking for love in all the wrong places, it was Thurmond.

"He set you up, Thurmond, from start to finish. He knew you better than you knew yourself, and you walked right into it. Take my advice; go back to your family."

"I don't have a family anymore," Thurmond said, and he started to cry.

Oh, for Christ's sake, thought Flynn.

"Then go on the gay cruise you were going on. You have it booked anyway. Maybe you'll meet someone on it."

"I guess this is yours then." He put the briefcase on Flynn's desk in front of Flynn.

Flynn pushed it to the side with his foot.

"Aren't you going to count it?"

"No. I trust you."

"So what do I do now?"

"You walk out of here, and walk down the street. On the corner is a gay bar. It's early, but there will be a few players around. Get good and drunk and watch your wallet. Thank your lucky stars because you missed a bullet the size of an RPG."

"Thanks, Flynn. I mean it."

Thurmond left and closed the door behind him. Flynn swiveled in his chair, so he was looking at the golden dome of the state's capital. It was built in the 1800's and Flynn always thought it was an impressive piece of architecture.

Later, as the shadows lengthened into afternoon, Flynn felt his ghost and mentor enter the room and sit down beside him.

"You've never let me down, Flynn, you know that?" His ghost said in his mind.

"Well, it was touch and go there for a while, wasn't it?" Flynn said aloud to the empty room.

"Not from my vantage point, it wasn't."

"I met your son. I decided not to tell him about you."

"I know."

"I think I did the right thing."

"You did the right thing, Flynn."

"How do you know?"

"Because we're all perfect imperfections. You're in this life to learn."

"What am I supposed to be learning?"

"What you've known all along, Flynn."

"James? I miss Mia. I need to talk to Mia and Mia Lynn."

"I'm proud of you, Flynn."

Flynn felt a hand on his shoulder, and he was once again left alone with his thoughts. He thought about getting drunk, but stopped himself.

He knew his ghost wouldn't approve.

"It is a man's own mind, not his enemy or foe, that lures him to evil ways."

Buddha

Chapter 25

Johnny Tran watched both Lamar and Flynn from a darkened window in a condo across the street.

After diving out the window, the first floor porch ledge broke his fall. He rolled off of that and dropped to the sidewalk in a 'tuck and roll' on the side opposite the front. He was half way across the street when he came out of his roll and kept on running into an alley next to a commercial condominium.

The close quarters' shotgun blast still rang in Johnny Tran's ears as he hid behind a dumpster. He wondered absently why he was alive. Some people came out of a side door to the condo. He took the opportunity to slip in past them as the door was closing.

He needed a place to hole up, watch what developed, and tend to his bruised and bleeding body. Tran forced all thoughts of pain from his mind.

He picked the condo directly across from the poker game and knocked on the door. An old woman answered the door. Her eyes went wide seeing the bloody apparition standing there.

It was the last thing she ever saw.

Tran drove the point of the katana into the soft spot below her Adam's apple, and out through the base of her skull, as he pushed her back into her house. He pulled the sword out and left her laying there, dying slowly in her own blood.

"Mildred? Who is it?"

"Your death, old man," Johnny Tran said, walking up to him.

"But why?"

"Because you have the bad Karma to meet me this night."

Johnny Tran dispatched old man quickly, and pushed him out of his chair. He hauled the chair to a more favorable position where he could watch the action across the way unseen.

Tran watched as Lamar pulled his face mask off and looked up and down the street. A large guy he didn't know joined him at the window and talked to Lamar. Tran could tell by the way they were talking, the big guy was a boss. Johnny Tran committed his face to memory.

There was a flurry of activity in the background, then two paramedics rushed out putting a gurney into an ambulance. That must be the foreigner who came late to the game. Johnny Tran was surprised he lived.

How had an ambulance gotten there so fast? He asked himself. Another man he didn't recognize got into the ambulance, and then the girl with the foreigner tried to get in. The paramedic tried to stop her and in a flash, he was down on the ground. The girl had him in a Ju Jitsu hand lock. Then she released him, helped him up, and both got into the ambulance. The ambulance sped away, sirens wailing.

It was a set up. The foreigner and his girlfriend were the plants. Lamar called in some outside help.

Which meant, Lamar had an inside informant.

Which meant, his organization was compromised.

Which meant, it was time to get rough.

Johnny Tran had what he needed to know. Now it was time to take stock of his injured body. He felt every ache, pain, and tingle in his body. He walked to the bathroom, stripped off his clothes, and started a shower. Once the blood of others had been washed off he could see the extent of his own injuries.

Tran caught some of the shot gun blast to his side. His other side was scraped raw from the contact with the ledge. He suspected, then confirmed by pressing his fingers into his side; some ribs were broken. He had numerous cuts from diving out the window, some quite deep.

Johnny looked around the bathroom, and as he suspected, the couple had an extensive first aid cabinet. He looked through the pills on the night stand in their bedroom and even found some painkillers.

Time to get to work.

Stopping the blood loss was Johnny's first concern. He used a needle and thread from the old woman's sewing kit, to sew up the largest gashes. Then Tran found some panty liners in a spare bedroom, soaked them in hydrogen peroxide, and taped them on to make a makeshift bandage.

Using a pair of tweezers and a magnifying makeup mirror, Johnny pulled as many pieces of buckshot out of his side as he could. Some he had to tease out with his fingers, rolling them from side to side and pushing them to the surface. Others never penetrated the outer layer of skin, and could be plucked out. He set his ribs the best he could, and wrapped himself with tape.

His leg was a separate problem. He could still use it, so he knew it wasn't broken. But walking unaided was out of the question. He used the katana as a make-shift splint for his leg. He could use the katana to take his weight instead of his leg. He taped it in place with the last of the duct-tape. He stood up on it. It worked, just barely. It worked enough to get out of there.

Waves of dizziness washed over Johnny as the last of his adrenaline ebbed from his system. He hobbled over to the spare bedroom and collapsed on the bed.

He'd first get some sleep, then he'd start planning his revenge.

"Some people would say comedy draws from some dark places, from your dark stuff. Life's great optimists aren't necessarily the funniest people."

Colin Firth

Chapter 26

"Do you want the good news, or the bad news?" the Doctor said to Wee.

Ning who had been standing protectively by Wee's hospital bed, all night, said, "We'll take the good news first."

Cobalt had eased in behind the doctor and was standing unobtrusively in the doorway.

"Is it okay if I speak with everyone present? HIPAA rules, and all. I have to ask."

"Yes, go ahead," said Wee weakly.

"First, your neck and shoulder. Your carotid artery was completely missed. A millimeter more and you wouldn't be here. Instead, it knicked your collarbone, and damaged the muscle and nerves of your shoulder. I was able to repair them. Second, I extracted 123 of buckshot out of your back, gluteus maximus, and thighs." The doctor held up a clear plastic tube, shaking it for effect, "I thought you might want it."

"What's my gluteus maximus?"

"Your ass, you idiot," Ning said.

"What's the bad news?"

"Your golf swing will never be the same," the surgeon said, smiling.

After the doctor left, Cobalt came forward. Ning, after keeping vigil all night, wanted to go to the cafeteria and get some coffee, so she left. The two men were left alone.

"Some bodyguard you turned out to be," Cobalt said with a quirky smile, "Do you make a habit of stepping in front of shotguns?"

"Did Flynn get Tran?"

"No, he got away."

"Figures. So I got cut up for nothing?"

"I wouldn't say that. You have Nurse Ning fussing over you. They've got to be giving you some good painkillers…"

"I hope Ning didn't go all momma hen on you. She gets that way…"

"She never left your side. Chop-sockied a paramedic when he didn't want to let her in the ambulance. How did you guys meet, anyway?"

Here Wee paused, thinking back. Gone was the jester, with the idiotic smile. With the drugs letting his guard down, he revealed himself as a thinking, considerate, person.

"I joined the Army, as all Thai males are required to do and found I had a talent for guns. I was promoted to marksman, then to sniper. A shortage of heavy weapon's gunners appeared and this was a new way of applying my talent, so I volunteered."

"Is that how you met Ning?"

"No," Wee laughed, "Captain Ning rescued me later." Wee automatically reverted back to rank and professional discipline when recalling.

"Rescued? Interesting choice of words."

"It happened like this; in late 2008 Thai and Cambodia got into another dispute over the Preah Vihear temple complex on the Eastern border. It was typical government posturing and bullshit. No one thought it would turn hot. But I was forward deployed to the region. In early 2009 it did turn hot when three Thai soldiers were killed.

"I was with a machine gun unit when one of my buddies stepped on a land mine. The situation went to shit fast. The Thai's believed that the Cambodians fired on them. The Cambodians believed we started it. I was there and I don't know who started what. All I know was my buddy lost a leg and I had to get him out of there.

"We called in air support, and none would come. We called in a medical evac chopper, and no one would take him out as it as considered too dangerous. That was when all hell broke loose. Tracers were going everywhere, but mostly over our heads. I still believe the Cambodians weren't trying to kill us, just scare us. Otherwise why fire over our heads?"

"Okay, I know what you mean," said Cobalt.

"I applied a tourniquet to my buddy's leg and hunkered down.

That's when a Huey came in fast and low, under considerable fire. I mean, the Cambos saw it and just lit it up. The pilot must have seen me, or seen the blood, because he landed that bird as close as possible. The cargo door opened, and the door gunner laid down suppressing fire. That's when I knew, I wanted to be THAT guy."

Wee drifted off into past reverie, eyes unfocused, staring into the past…

"Go, go GO!" The door gunner yelled at Wee.

Wee grabbed his friend's arm, hoisted him up, and onto his shoulder in fireman's carry. Bullets kicked up around Wee's feet and the door gunner jumped on the big double .50 caliber again, laying down suppressing fire. Wee almost got to the chopper when he caught a bullet in the upper thigh and down he went.

The door gunner jumped from the chopper, and went to help Wee, which meant, no one was laying down return fire. Bullets whacked into the chopper left and right; some cracked the windshield as a Cambodian officer obviously ordered his men to try and take out the pilot. The pilot took the bird up a few feet off the ground and turned it around in a 180 degree turn.

Now the other door gunner came into play, and the chopper pilot was no longer facing the enemy. The tail rotor was exposed, however.

The first door gunner reached Wee, grabbed him and started hauling Wee toward the chopper. He got Wee into the chopper and then went to get his buddy.

"Leave him! Leave him! It's too hot. We can't stay!" said the other door gunner.

The pilot looked back at Wee, saw the look in his eyes, and nodded. "We leave no one behind," the look said. Quiet orders delivered, and carried out. Wee could see the bullet holes in the windshield all around the pilot's seat. Both door gunners jumped out and retrieved Wee's friend, hauling him into the chopper.

"What happened then?" asked Cobalt.

"We returned to base. My friend lost his leg, but lived. And I have a hole in my ass."

"Didn't you have a hole in your ass before joining the army?" said Cobalt, smiling in jest.

"Shut up, Cobalt, this is my story."

"Okay, okay," said Cobalt, amused, interested despite himself. "Who was the pilot?"

"Will you let me finish? I'm getting to that part."

"A few days later, the door gunner came to visit in the hospital. He just dropped in to see how we were doing. After all, he risked his life, he didn't want to see us die."

"Yeah, that really would have been bad manners on your part," said Cobalt, deadpan.

"After the door gunner came a doctor, and what I thought was a specialist. I tell you Cobalt, she was so good looking it made getting shot in the ass worth it."

"I thought you said you got shot in the thigh?"

"Don't quibble over minor details, Cobalt, it's unseemly."

"Oh, right,"

" Anyway, the doctor came up and said 'This is Captain Ning,' I nodded hello. I still thought she was a doctor."

The door gunner looked up, stood immediately, and saluted.

"Captain Ning is the pilot who pulled your sorry ass out of that rice paddy," said the doctor. Wee noticed then the gauze bandage just inside Captain Ning's hairline. She was wounded herself.

"I tell you Cobalt, I knew right then and there. I was going to be her door gunner until death do us part."

"So what happened then? I mean, did you get down on your hands and knees and worship at the Temple of Ning?"

"No, but I got a medal for getting shot in the ass and a month off with pay."

"Almost as good," said Cobalt, smiling.

"Worship at the 'Temple of Ning'? Is that what I heard you say Cobalt?" Ning asked, standing in the doorway, listening silently to the story. "Of course, he did," she came into the room and put her arm around Wee. "And he has ever since. I have that effect on people. Wee knows a class act when he sees one."

"Class act, my ass," Wee said, grinning idiotically, back to his old self. "Cobalt, did I ever tell you the first time I met Ning, she was a crack whore on Soi Cowboy in Bangkok?"

"You have enemies? Good. That means you've stood up for something, sometime in your life."

Winston Churchill

Chapter 27

The next morning, Flynn was back in the cab, following Johnny Tran, and trying to learn his routine.

Any successful operation depends on good intelligence, which in this case, meant knowing everything about his target.

Driving a cab had its advantages and disadvantages. He could drive around and be fairly invisible day or night. He could surveil targets, follow them, and one taxi looked just like all the others. The disadvantage was sometimes people hopped in his cab and expected him to drive them. Most the time he could get out of it just by saying, "off duty" and they would flag down another cab.

Tran during the day was Johnny Tran businessman. The Samurai sword was replaced with an Armani business suit. No doubt he still carried the small knife under his arm. He made the rounds to his businesses, and for all the world looked like he was solving the problems of businessmen the world over.

Flynn walked in behind him on a couple of occasions during lunch at his restaurants. Unlike businessmen the world over, the business owners didn't have a look of abject fear when they saw their banker.

Johnny Tran would shake their hands, smile, and tell a joke while leading them to the back rooms.

Flynn was led to a table but at the last minute decided on take-out, so he could get back to his cab. He ordered spring rolls and Bun Bo Hue soup.

Flynn finished his last spring roll when Johnny Tran climbed into the back of his cab.

"I want to know why you are following me," Johnny Tran, said.

Either he had been tipped off, or he was a lot more observant than Flynn gave him credit for.

"Sorry pal," putting on his best cabbie attitude, "but I got better things to do than follow you around. No harm, no foul, all cabs look the same, I guess."

"Then you won't mind taking me to Second Avenue"

"Sure, no problem." He wanted to go to Viet town.

Flynn hit the meter, and they drove in silence.

"So what do you do?" Flynn asked to break the silence.

"I'm a business owner."

"Really? You own that restaurant we just left? Best spring rolls in town."

Tran pulled out a cell phone, made a call, and ignored the question.

"So where to on Second Avenue?" Flynn asked after he finished the call.

"Triple Dragon market."

Flynn cruised down the street, then hung a left into the parking lot.

"Nine dollars and twenty-five cents."

Instead of getting out of the cab, two more Vietnamese males entered, one in back, and one in front. They had their hands inside their coats, but didn't pull out weapons.

"Look, I don't want any trouble," Flynn said, reaching down the driver's door for his 9mm automatic, fully expecting trouble and ready for it.

"No, you don't," Johnny Tran said, "But take this tip," he slid a one hundred-dollar bill over the front seat, "And I'll give you another tip, worth even more. I don't ever want to see you again."

What Flynn didn't know was that Johnny Tran recognized him standing at the window with Lamar on the night of the botched raid on the poker game.

The hunter just became the hunted.

"Tact is the art of making a point without making an enemy."

Isaac Newton

Chapter 28

"I think Johnny Tran know I talked to you. I'm in big trouble."

Tram Ngoc, the Vietnamese nail tech that told Flynn about when and where the girls were being unloaded, burst into Flynn east side office, in tears.

"Why do you think that? Did he say anything?"

"No. The Vietnamese way is not to say anything. You have to, how you Americans say? 'Read between lines.'"

"Okay, so what did you read between the lines?"

"It is in the way he look at me."

"Which was…?"

"Like I am a bug he is about to step on."

Flynn looked at her closely for the first time. She was very pretty, between twenty and twenty-five. Long dark hair, and milk chocolate colored skin. She was wearing a sleeveless blouse, and had the slender, flawless arms and shoulders of a young girl.

"Why didn't you go see Lamar? Couldn't he help you better than I can?"

"I tried, he say come see you."

Flynn sighed. This was a complication he didn't need. He could no longer surveil Johnny Tran without attracting unwanted attention, or worse. Which meant he had no idea what he was doing, or planning. This put Flynn at a severe disadvantage. A disadvantage he was that minute trying to figure out.

His next-best option was to put a transmitter on Tran's car. However, for that to work, he needed to know which car Tran was driving. So far, he couldn't pick up a pattern or determine a car that was his. He usually had other people drive him. He had no cars registered to him, or any real estate in his name. So Flynn also had no idea where he lived.

"Please," Tram Ngoc said, getting down on her hands and knees. She wiggled her way between Flynn's legs and the message was clear. "I think he is going to kill me." Flynn had a clear shot down her blouse to perfect breasts.

"Please," she said, again, crying softly. "I stay here. I take care of you. Anything you want, I do."

Flynn, like all men, hated crying females. It was their gender's secret weapon; it worked like a charm, and they knew it.

"That's not necessary," Flynn said, trying to lift her up and away from his crotch, which was swelling against his will. "I'll help you if I can."

"I can't go back."

"Why not?"

"It is too dangerous. I might never get away again."

"What if your radar is wrong?"

"I don't understand 'radar'…"

"What if your feeling about Johnny Tran is wrong? If you don't go back, he will know something is wrong. He will come looking for you. If he finds you here, he will kill you absolutely."

"Why would he come here? He knows nothing of you."

"He knows now because yesterday he visited me in my cab."

Tram just looked at Flynn in horror.

"Oh no, no, no….What am I going to do?"

"I'm not sure yet. But you can stay here while I talk to Lamar and get this straightened out."

Tram got up and went and sat in a chair on the other side of the desk. Head down, defeated. Flynn pushed a button on the underside of his desk and a video camera started rolling silently. Flynn would know everything she did in his office while he was gone.

Flynn may have liked her, but that didn't mean he trusted her.

"We need to meet," Flynn said to Lamar, as soon as he left his office.

"What up?"

"Your girl came to see me."

"Could you be a little more specific? I do have more than one in my employ."

"The Vietnamese," Not wanting to say her name on the phone.

"Oh, she a beauty, isn't she?"

"She said you sent her to me."

"That so?"

"Lamar, for Christ's sake…I need to know if I'm being played."

"If you are, she be a good one to play with."

"Do you believe her?"

"I believed her enough to send her to you," Lamar said, and burst out laughing.

"If you want her in your stable, why don't you take her?"

"Well, because if what she say is true, then that would lead Johnny Tran to me, wouldn't it?"

"Right, so it is much better to lead him to me, is that it?"

"It is from where I be standing."

"You asshole…"

"Just want to make sure my peoples is properly motivated. Now you stay healthy and don't be accepting no wooden nickels or fake Samurai swords."

Flynn walked to his cab, going the long way around the entire block, looking for anything out of place. He saw only the usual businessmen and women and early evening party-goers. He walked on to the parking garage where he stored his cab. Hopped in the front seat and plugged his laptop into the cigarette lighter. He booted it up then picked up the wireless signal from the video. Tram was no longer sitting in the chair where he left her.

He rewound the video until he saw himself leave, then hit play from there.

Tram Ngoc sat in his office alone. He could see her shoulders move up and down as she cried. Then she got up and moved over to his couch, where she curled up and went to sleep.

Flynn didn't see, and didn't know, that while she was on her knees between his legs, she opened the fabric under his chair with her fingernail, and planted a listening device, hidden inside the torn fabric.

Nor did he see her planting the drugs in the seat cushion as she was laying on the couch.

"If you want to make enemies, try to change something
for the better"

Woodrow Wilson

Chapter 29

The beat down came the next morning when Flynn left his office.

The ambush was perfectly laid. Flynn made a habit of looking up and down the street while exiting his office to scanning for threats, before stepping out onto the sidewalk. He was especially alert this morning, after Tram Ngoc spent the night on the couch upstairs. Not seeing, or sensing, any threat, he continued to the parking garage.

His cab was parked in a row of cars, and he sensed movement as he put the key in the door lock. His attacker popped up from in front of his cab where he had been invisible. He carried a set of nun-chuks, doing a Bruce Lee across his front and back.

Dipshit, thought Flynn.

Dipshit or no, Nun-Chuk went straight into attack.

Flynn loved his yellow checker cab for lots of reasons, but one of the best reasons was that it was built like a tank. It was made for heavy, inner-city use. It also had a number of refinements Flynn had added over the years.

Flynn had about two seconds to defend himself, the time it took for his assailant to cover the distance between the front of the cab to the driver's door. The nun-chuck swinging on its short chain, shortened the time span to about one second. It was barely enough time to duck the first swing.

In the time it took to duck, Flynn got the door opened. His attacker was at the rear of the front fender now and closing fast, nun-chuks a swinging blur of hardwood. If one connected, it would break his head open. Flynn ducked and got his hand into the opened car door. He then used it as a battering ram, hitting his attacker and ducking behind the open door while reaching into the door compartment for his pistol, keeping the door as a barrier between his attacker and himself. He didn't reach the pistol in time.

Which meant Flynn didn't see the tough with a bicycle chain come up behind him.

Flynn caught the movement behind him out of the corner of his eye, but not fast enough to stop the chain from biting into his neck and shoulder. It opened up his shoulder and wrapped around his neck, as tough number two yanked him backwards away from his gun.

Flynn did a back roll and came up directly in front of his surprised attacker's face, then head butted him as hard as he could. His forehead connected to cartilage and his attackers nose immediately gushed blood as he reeled backwards.

Nun-Chuc was still trying to get past the door separating them. Flynn let him unjam the door and try and squeeze between the door and the car next to it. Then he drove his body weight forward and rammed the door again, this time as the thug was halfway through the opening, the door caught him where his legs met his torso all the way up to his forehead.

Unable to move from between the door, with the door bisecting his body, rendered his nun-chuks useless. Flynn took the moment to slam the door repeatedly against his attacker until he collapsed.

Bicycle Chain was now coming back to his senses and advancing towards Flynn, swinging the bicycle chain in wide arcs.

Oh, fuck this, thought Flynn. He grabbed his 9mm from the door compartment and shot Bicycle Chain once in the kneecap. The sound was huge in the enclosed space of the cement garage. The first shot missed, of course. The adrenaline spiking through his body throwing his aim off. The second shot didn't miss, though. Bicycle Chain still had time to wrap the chain around the side of Flynn's head, shredding his face, before he went down. Flynn was going to have another facial scar to add to his growing collection.

Flynn saw stars and collapsed.

A passing car saw the melee and called 911. Nun-Chuk was coming to, so with the last burst of energy he had, Flynn disarmed him, and laid the hardwood cylinder of the nun-chuk square down on the top of his head, cracking his head open and knocking him unconscious.

Flynn heard sirens closing in on the parking garage and didn't want to spend time telling long-winded stories down at the police station about what had just transpired.

Let them figure it out.

Bicycle Chain heard the sirens too and agreed with Flynn about explaining to the cops and was trying to crawl off, dragging his useless leg behind him. Flynn kicked him a solid one in the side of the head to put a stop to those ambitions, then took the stairs and made it back to his office without attracting attention.

When he got back to his office, Tram Ngoc was gone.

"Lots of people want to ride with you in the limo, but what you want is someone who will take the bus with you when the limo breaks down.

Oprah Winfrey

Chapter 30

Flynn collapsed into his chair and reached for some Tylenol to deaden the pain in his face.

He flipped open his cell phone and could think of only one person to call. His vision was going in and out and he knew he had a mild concussion. In addition, he felt like puking from the adrenaline ebbing from his system.

He dialed Ning's number.

"Missed me?" She picked up on the first ring.

"It depends on if you have any medical skills."

"I'm trained in battlefield first aid, yes," she said seriously.

"Good. I need you to stitch up my face."

"Where are you?"

"My office."

"Be there in fifteen."

Flynn passed the time by reviewing the office video of Tram Ngoc after he left that morning. She got up, made some tea heating hot water using the coffee maker, fished around in her purse for some Korean Ginseng tea, and let it steep. While it steeped, she took her blouse off, and treated Flynn once again to her perfect breasts, then took one of Flynn's clean shirts from the closet. It was comically large on her small frame, and hung almost to her knees. She somehow managed to roll it up, tie it under her breasts, and ended up looking incredibly sexy.

She drank her tea, and walked out the door.

Ning arrived on time, minus any bodyguards this time. She glanced at the computer which was frozen on Tram Ngoc, half naked, reaching her arms over her head, stretching in the morning sunlight.

"You want to watch out for those little Vietnamese hell-cats the morning after. They don't take rejection well," she said, not overly perturbed.

"Now, she tells me."

"Those don't look like claw marks to me."

"They aren't. Wrong end of a bicycle chain."

Ning sat on the edge of the desk, turning Flynn's head this way and that, examining the wound.

"Want to talk about it?"

"Not really."

"You keep any medical supplies around here?"

"Yeah, over there in the cabinet."

Ning walked over to the cabinet, looked through what was available, and took out what she needed. She walked back, pushed the laptop out of the way, and spread the supplies over the desktop.

"I've got to clean this up first."

Flynn made a 'knock yourself out' gesture. Ning used hydrogen peroxide to clean the wound. The peroxide immediately started to bubble and hiss as it bit into the bacteria. She wiped it off and squeezed the wound shut with her fingers, causing more blood to be expelled, which she wiped off again with gauze.

"You know, that does hurt," Flynn said, trying not to flinch.

"Aww, poor baby. It's going to hurt even more when I start stitching."

Flynn watched her thread the semi-circular suture needle like a pro.

"Hold still."

Ning sat on the desktop and had to get in close to Flynn's face. Her breath smelled like cloves, and her hair smelled like jasmine. Flynn was swooning in the various fragrances when the pain from piercing both sides of his wound drove all thoughts of sex out of his mind.

"If you've got painkillers I'll use them, but they make the scar bigger."

"Just stitch it up."

Flynn closed his eyes and tried to think of more pleasant things, which wasn't hard because Ning's breasts kept rubbing against his arm and he could feel the warm, soft, fullness pressing against him.

She closed his face with twelve expert sutures, so close together the scarring would be minimal. Flynn just gutted his way through the pain by mentally undressing her.

"I heard chicks dig scars, is it true?" Flynn asked Ning when she was finished, as she was examining her handiwork.

"Well, Frankenstein, it depends. A scar here or there adds some character. But looking the way you do, like Leather Face in the 'Texas Chainsaw Massacre' leaves a bit to be desired. Sorry, but my mom wouldn't approve." Ning said, smiling.

"So, you'll be taking me home to meet your parents? Before or after the wedding?"

"Maybe we should try coffee first, before sending out any invitations…"

Three hard, loud, raps boomed on the door at that moment.

"Police! Open up."

Flynn and Ning looked at each other.

"Do you need to get rid of any incriminating evidence?"

"No, this about the two idiots I left bleeding on the floor of the parking garage. It happened next to my cab. I'm sure they ran the plates."

"What do you want me to do?"

"Nothing. Act sweet and innocent, since you are."

"Flynn! Open the door, or we're taking it down!"

"Okay, okay, I'm coming," Flynn yelled to the cops outside.

Flynn unlocked a series of dead bolts, and unshot two large bolts at the top, and bottom, of the door. He opened the door and was immediately spun around and pushed face first against the wall and handcuffed as a SWAT team forced their way inside.

The TAC team was in body armor with their faces covered.

"Is this necessary? I'm an ex-cop. We're not resisting."

Flynn was shoved back into the office and he could see Ning was down on the floor with her hands behind her head and her ankles crossed. An officer had a knee in her back as he brought her arms down to handcuff her. Another officer stood over her with MP5 submachine gun, his finger on the trigger. Something that was against police SOP once a suspect was secured.

"Shut up," the commanding officer said, forcing Flynn to his knees. "Cross your ankles."

Once secured, they were left on the floor, face down, as police swarmed over the office. One cop made a bee-line to the couch, rooted around like he knew exactly where to go, and came up holding a small plastic bag containing white powder.

"You have the right to remain silent…" another masked SWAT team member said, hauling them both to their feet, and marching them out the door.

Johnny Tran sat across the street in a condo he rented the day before in order to keep an eye on Flynn. He listened to the transmitter sending audio of the conversations, as well as watched the excitement through the patio doors. He sat well back in the shadows, so he wouldn't be seen.

"Corruption is worse than prostitution. The latter might endanger the morals of an individual, the former invariably endangers the morals of the entire country."

Karl Kraus

Chapter 31

When you have corrupt cops, all things are possible.

Flynn and Ning were loaded into separate cars. Ning looked at Flynn, hoping for a clue as to how to react, but Flynn just shook his head. 'Don't say a word', his look said. Their heads were pushed into the cars at the same time, and that was the last she saw of him. She was taken downtown, and put in an interrogation room to stew.

Flynn's mind was racing. He didn't do drugs, so he knew they weren't his. He knew Tram Ngoc had planted them. Not that the cops would care. It was a felony bust with intent to distribute. They had the goodies. That was all they needed for an arrest.

Flynn also knew he had a few friends left in the department from the old days, but most of the cops now were a new generation of storm troopers. They watched too many episodes of TV's 'Cops' and liked the military weapons the federal government had been throwing at them for the last ten years.

Cops always had an "Us vs. Them" mentality when it came to doing their job. But lately, with the militarization of police, the 'Them' included everyone, criminals and citizens alike. Cops these days didn't distinguish between good guys and bad guys. Everyone was a bad guy, and it was their job to take them all down if they got caught in the cross hairs of law enforcement.

Flynn was led to an interrogation room and told to sit down. His handcuffs were taken off and one wrist was cuffed to the table.

Flynn knew the routine. He would be left here for a few hours while the cops collected as much incriminating evidence against him as they could. He was supposed to stew over his sins and be reduced to a bawling baby by the time they came back to pepper him with half truths, guesses, and outright lies to get him to incriminate himself further prior to booking.

Flynn had some guesses, half-truths, and outright lies of his own.

"They don't write, they don't call…" A detective said, coming into the room.

"McDuff, you still around? I thought they shit-canned you right after me."

"My, my, someone really seems to have taken a dislike to your face, Flynn. Of course, most people take a dislike to your face once they get to know you."

Down the hall, in another interrogation room, the same drill was being played out with Ning.

"Felony drugs. Intent to distribute. How long you think she'll get? Ten years? Then what? Deportation would be my guess. A good looking girl like you, spending the best years of her life behind bars. A shame, a real shame. Do you have anything to say before we do a strip search?"

"Yes."

"We know the drugs weren't yours. Flynn was caught dirty, red-handed years ago. It comes as no surprise he'd be dealing drugs now. Just tell us what we need to know and you can walk. We don't want you."

"Okay. Here's what you need to know; I want a lawyer."

That was the last word they heard her say.

"So how'd you get that cat-scratch, Flynn?"

"A cat scratched me."

"Yeah, some cats have sharp claws."

"And some have deep pockets, too. Isn't that right, McDuff?"

"Are you insinuating something?"

"Hell no. It's common knowledge."

"You're a fine one to talk Flynn. Sucking Jeffery Prescott's cock all those years. How'd that work out for you anyway? I heard you took it up the ass."

"I'm willing to bet you'll take it up the ass as soon as I pull down

Johnny Tran and expose your ties to him."

The detective's eyes narrowed.

Bingo!

"Oh, that was not smart, McDuff. You should play those games on citizens who don't understand how things work. You know as well as I do, there's always a trail. Even if there isn't a trail, then there is some citizen shooting incriminating video. So I'm going to take a wild stab in the dark here, okay McDuff?"

"As usual, Flynn. Talking shit."

"Like I said, a wild stab in the dark. If I remember right, you were reprimanded for doing some young thing in your cruiser. I bet Tran supplies all the young ones you want, doesn't he? Is it true pedophilia is a life long addiction? One that can't be cured?"

"You got a big mouth, Flynn," McDuff said, dangerously. But he walked over and unplugged the video recording the interrogation.

Full house, jokers wild! Flynn was on a roll.

"Really? I'm just getting warmed up. Did I tell you I'm a big fan of wireless video? I have my office wired with video, on a motion detector no less. So I know what goes on in my office even when I'm not there. I can prove someone planted those drugs. I also had the alley wired with video the night Tran took that load of girls behind the Dac Biet restaurant. Guess who I saw show up and take some merchandise off the truck? Guess who has video of the whole transaction?"

"So I'll shake this charge, if you're stupid enough to try to book me, we both know it. After all, we both know how this works. I have information to trade. But here's what I promise you. I will make it my mission in life to connect you to Johnny Tran, to his network of underage girls, and the police on his payroll. Not only will Internal Affairs get a copy of the video, but I'll make sure Action Channel News gets one too, just to get IA moving in the right direction. You know I can do it, too, McDuff."

"So what are you suggesting?"

"He paid you to roust me and bust me, which you did. The SWAT team was a nice touch. You got your jollies. He got his point across. You keep me in this holding cell for a few more hours while you figure out how to lose that heroin or cocaine or whatever it was, then you let me and my friend go, citing lack of evidence or whatever technicality you want to cite."

Flynn and Ning walked out of the station twelve hours later.

"Political Correctness doesn't change us, it shuts us up."

Glenn Beck

Chapter 32

Lo Chin didn't like coming to the United States.

Even though he had an American passport, he preferred living outside the country. Being old school, all the political correctness bullshit bothered him. He no longer knew if what he did, or said, even when being polite, was acceptable. The cultural rules in US changed as fast as his underwear.

Furthermore, the indignity of dealing with the TSA deeply offended him. The TSA reminded him of the petty bureaucrats in Asia. Little people in life, who once given a taste of power over others, had to prove how powerful they were every chance they got.

Last, the flights were unbearably long on his aging body. While he preferred the anonymity of flying coach, the lack of leg room made such a long flight impossible. He shook his head. American airlines used to be the best in the world. Now they were the worst. He preferred the Korean or Thai airlines now.

He flew into LAX after a thirteen-hour flight across the Pacific. Customs and Immigration were professional at least. He boarded another flight, and it took an additional twelve hours to cover two thousand miles of the interior USA to Des Moines, with a two-hour layover in Denver.

He arrived in Des Moines and looked at his watch. Time-wise, it had only been one hour since he left Vietnam. In reality, twenty-five hours passed. The time zone differences flying East to West never failed to screw up his internal clock for days afterward.

He got his bags and walked out into the Iowa sunshine. The weather was cool and crisp, such a change from sweltering Vietnam. A black limo slid to the curb, and a driver got out to open the door. Johnny Tran was already inside.

"It's good to see you, Grandfather."

Lo Chin nodded but said nothing. The flight left him exhausted. Jet lag was settling in. Instead he looked out the smoked glass as they drove up Fleur Drive towards downtown. His room at the Embassy Suites was ready when he arrived. After settling in, tipping the bell hop, and ordering room service, Lo Chin was ready to discuss the business at hand.

"Let me see the intelligence you have collected, please."

Johnny Tran had anticipated this request and handed over the dossier.

Lo Chin read quietly, then closed the folder, and leaned back on the settee.

"It seems you have two problems, not just one, and possibly a third." Lo Chin said quietly.

"The dark skin can be dealt with easily once the white skin is neutralized."

"He is police. This is not Vietnam. In Vietnam, we can pay the police off. Here it is trickier and best not to involve them unless we have leverage."

"He is ex-police. Not on the force anymore. Disgraced."

"He will have friends still in positions of power. I see you've already tried intimidation as well as setting him up with no success. Can he be blackmailed?"

"I don't see how. He is careful now. We sent one of the girls over to see if he would succumb to sex, but he was smart enough not to. Instead, we planted a listening device as well as the drugs in his office."

"The drug set up didn't work either?"

"No."

"What do you suggest?"

"We have two choices. We can up the intimidation factor and send a strong warning. He may back off if he understands the true cost of doing business with us."

"If that doesn't work?" Lo Chin asked.

"We have no choice but to resort to extreme measures, which is why I wanted your approval first."

"We exist here by remaining out of sight," Lo Chin said, rubbing his eyes. "This kind of action risks calling attention to ourselves. A cockroach may be a cockroach, but he has survived millions of years by hiding in the cracks. He doesn't come out into the light for a reason. The reason is he gets stomped on very quickly if he does. He has adapted. He knows the best time to feed is when no one is looking."

"I understand Grandfather, but this police is a cockroach too. He also hides in the shadow of society. He is not out in the full light either. He is not a citizen. He has no family. His friends are few. If he gets stomped on, few people will miss this cockroach."

There was a knock on the door. Johnny Tran got up and answered it. It was room service. Instead of letting the porter in, Johnny tipped him and took the service cart there in the doorway. The fewer people who saw Lo Chin, the better.

"Come, Grandfather, it is time to eat."

Business conversation was dropped as both men sat down to the meal. One of the best things about the USA, thought Lo Chin, was the quality of the meat. The beef in Vietnam was not even worth eating. He had to import his steak. US beef, while not as good as Japanese or Argentinian beef, was also much cheaper than both. What it lacked in quality it made up for in price. One of the high points of any trip to America was eating a rib-eye steak.

When both men had finished their meal and were sitting over coffee, business conversation resumed.

"I think in this situation, intimidation should be stepped up," Lo Chin said, sipping his coffee.

"If that doesn't work"

"Then we will need to kidnap him quietly, and he will need to disappear."

"Terrorism is a psychological warfare. Terrorists try to manipulate us and change our behavior by creating fear, uncertainty, and division in society."

Patrick J. Kennedy

Chapter 33

The package came and was left on Flynn's doorstep.

There was nothing unusual about it. It was an Amazon box with the familiar logo and a curved arrow leading to a green "Buy Now" button. It was roughly the size of a hat box. Flynn carried it in and sat it on his desk. He hadn't ordered any books from Amazon, so he wasn't expecting anything.

The package was oddly heavy and over sized for books. Amazon sold lots of different products so it didn't come across as odd.

Flynn used his pocket knife and slit the top of the box. He opened the outer cardboard folds. Inside, the box was stuffed with paper filler. Flynn noticed some strands of dark hair on the brown paper, and unease crept into his gut.

Flynn used the edge of his knife to remove the rest of the paper. Not wanting to contaminate a crime scene was a habit from his days on the police force.

Tram Ngoc's severed head was lying in the bottom of the box.

There was a note stapled to her forehead. It read,

"Quit while you 'a head.'"

"Violence does, in truth, recoil upon the violent, and the schemer falls into the pit which he digs for another."

Arthur Conan Doyle

Chapter 34

The death of Tram Ngoc hit Flynn hard. He didn't even know why.

It wasn't like she was a friend, or even someone close to Flynn. She had set him up to take the fall for illegal drugs she planted in his office. Not exactly the basis for a lasting relationship. Still, Flynn felt himself falling into a depression.

Flynn knew in his heart he was a warrior. He carried the invisible mark on him. As such he was barred from certain social circles. Other people, citizens, sensed it and grew uncomfortable around him…until they needed him.

That was the price for being a warrior. It meant you were exiled to the border lands of society. An outback area populated by outlaws and adrenaline junkies. Those who knew true violence could never go back.

Hollywood never showed the true reality of violence. There was nothing glorious about it. It was ugly, dirty, and most of the time, senseless.

On seeing the severed head, Flynn's adrenaline spiked. He immediately went into combat mode. But there was nothing and no one to fight. All his senses went into high alert. Time expanded and contracted. Even his very breath seemed to take ten minutes to exhale. When he realized there was no fight, no danger, he collapsed mentally and internally, the same as he would after a fight to the death.

Here is what Hollywood doesn't show:

Physically, aside from any injuries you might have received, you're exhausted and sore. Every nerve ending is literally on fire, because every fiber of your being is screaming in bloody terror. You get the shakes, sometimes so bad you can't even hold a glass in your hand. Some people literally get sick to their stomachs and vomit, others shit themselves.

Mentally, you're even more of a mess. Part of you is screaming inside your head that you almost got your ass killed. Another part of your brain is reeling with revulsion at the things you did to survive. Your brain is jumping and short circuiting, because every nerve wants to talk at once.

Then the pain hits. The adrenaline ebbs, and suddenly you can feel every cut, scratch, ache, pressure or temperature. Depending on how badly you were injured, this can be completely disconcerting even if you weren't hurt, or screaming in agony if you were.

One of the most unexpected responses to violence, which is a totally human response effecting both men and women, you get hornier than a dog in heat. You will literally fuck anything in sight. That is why battlefield rapes occur so often.

Flynn once knew a cop, a decorated veteran of the SWAT team who took himself off active duty because he got a raging hard-on and ejaculated every time he pulled the trigger on a sniper rifle. He was sane enough to know this was an unhealthy response to a serious situation. Instead of getting more medals, he went and got psychiatric help.

The psychic wounds are deeper, and last longer, than the physical ones.

In the movies, a guy gets shot, there is a neat round hole, a little blood escapes, and he falls over dead.

Cops know different.

Dying bodies twitch, kick, strangle, gurgle and bleed. Cops see the bloody, mangled meat of the exit wound in what was once a breathing, living person.

They smell the sickening stench of violence, up close and personal. In addition to the smell of blood and intestinal chaos, dying bodies lose control of their bladders and sphincters too. They are covered in piss and shit.

Oh yeah, really glamorous.

These were the emotions going through Flynn as the afternoon deepened, casting shadows from the State Capital dome into his office. Flynn lay curled up on the floor, arms tightly hugging his knees, rocking back and forth, trying to get rid of the demons.

Flynn knew he was in the grip of extreme terror. Even with no im-mediate threat, he was still in combat mode. With visible effort he tried to get the shakes under control. That didn't work, but he succeeded in blowing his lunch. He got to the wastebasket in time, but half of his meal went all over his shirt anyway. Then he had the sickening stench of his own vomit wafting up to his nostrils.

Flynn wanted a drink. He hadn't had a drink in four years, since the Prescott mess, but he needed one now. He didn't quit drinking, so much as found, that as his conversations with James Cobalt increased, he no longer wanted to. He staggered to the cabinet where he kept the alcohol. Sometimes clients wanted it and he kept it on hand for them. He knew he wouldn't be able to hold a glass steady so he took the bottle.

Flynn took a long pull of the whiskey and felt the burn going all the way down. It made him puke, burning all the way back up again.

"Christ," he said out loud to the empty room, "what a loser you are."

It was at that moment that calmness flooded him, a certain "cen-teredness" entered his being, settling in the pit of his stomach, and he knew James Cobalt had entered the room.

"We fear violence less than our own feelings. Personal, private, solitary pain is more terrifying than what anyone else can inflict."

Jim Morrison

Chapter 35

"You going to eat your gun, Flynn?" Flynn's Ghost asked.

Flynn's ghost went and took a seat. In one sense, Flynn was ashamed that his ghost saw him in this condition. It was unseemly, to be shaking in the corner, covered in his own puke.

"You saw me with the back of my head blown out and my brains on the floor." Cobalt said, replying to the feeling in his mind, *"This is a piece of cake."*

"I don't know what came over me," Flynn said.

"I do. It's one thing to be a young warrior. It still affects you, but you're able to bounce back quicker. It's another thing to be an old combat veteran. The carnage stays with you. It takes longer to recover. The voices of the dead, both friends and enemies, become louder, and stay longer. It's the reason the armed forces like retiring you around forty. You're no longer the fighting machine you once were."

"I didn't even know her. Why do I care?"

"It not about her, Flynn. It's about you."

"What about me?"

"Well, obviously, something is causing an imbalance in your life. I've told you before, your head, your heart, and your actions must be congruent. If they aren't then you won't achieve long term happiness."

The shadows deepened into night. Flynn didn't bother turning on any lights. He still sat on the floor in the corner, with his arms around his knees.

"How did you know it was time to die?" Flynn asked his ghost.

"I could feel it in the pit of my existence that it was the right thing to do."

"I feel that way now."

"No you don't. That's the whiskey talking."

"How do you know?"

"Because if you truly felt that way, you'd have eaten your gun and we'd be having this discussion on a different plane."

"You're so comforting."

"I'm not here to comfort you."

"Why are you here?"

"To help you through a crisis in your soul."

"I don't like who I am anymore. I'm tired of the dreams that don't go away, the night sweats, and the screams."

"Then change who you are."

"I am, who I am."

"Oh, like Popeye the Sailor Man?"

"You know what I mean. How do I change who I am?"

"By first deciding who you want to be."

"Then?"

"Becoming who you decide to be."

"You make it sound so easy."

"It is easy. You're making it complicated."

"Easy for you, maybe. You're dead."

"All reality is first born by an idea. Before something can become reality, you have to think it into existence. It does not happen magically. First, you must have the idea of who you want to become. Then you have to figure out how to bring the person you want to be, into your present reality. Last, it will be created by reality. You have done the same thing in your life many times already."

"By wishing it were true?"

"Don't be an idiot and quit feeling sorry for yourself. It's more sickening than the puke on your shirt. Maybe it is time you found a home, and someone to go home to."

They talked long into the night.

Which is how Ning found Flynn the next morning, still sitting in the corner.

"You're a mess. What happened?" She saw the same look on the faces of men coming back from combat. She knew if he didn't return to the Land of the Living soon, he could get lost wandering in the Land of Suffering and eventually lose his mind.

Flynn gestured to the box on his desk. The head was starting to decompose. Blow flies had had all night to feast and lay eggs. There would be maggots soon.

Ning drew back from the smell before she even got to the box. She looked at Flynn, then looked inside. Her expression didn't change.

"She did my nails," Ning said.

"She set me up for that drug bust."

Flynn expected Ning to run from the office. She comes over for coffee and sees the person she came for huddled in a puddle of puke and a severed head decomposing on his desk. The normal response of a female would be to get out of Dodge, and quickly.

"If we're going to have a conversation, then you're going to have to get cleaned up. You stink. So does that," she said, pointing to the box. "I'm not sure who stinks the worst."

Instead of running screaming out the door, she grabbed Flynn under the arms and lifted him up. She steadied him and brought him to the attached bathroom. Ning turned on the hot water and adjusted the spray.

"This works best if you take off your clothes before getting in the shower," she said.

Flynn made a half-hearted try at unbuttoning his shirt. Ning stepped in and undid the buttons.

"I'm throwing this away," she said, indicating the shirt.

She ran her fingers over the scars on Flynn's chest.

"A lot of pain, here."

Ning unzipped Flynn's pants, and pushed them down. Her hands were cool and soft. She raised each leg and pulled off each pant leg. With one smooth motion, she peeled his boxers off. Her hand drifted down to his cock.

"Are you going to scrub my back, too?" Flynn said, hardening.

She held Flynn's cock in her hand, gently stroking it, knowing he needed the release of sex to come back to the living. Flynn held back for as long as he could, which wasn't long, and ejaculated.

"Maybe another time," she said.

"I'd like that."

"I'd like that, too."

"Max Cobalt said you started this life as a boy, is that true?"

"Max has a big mouth."

"Yes, but is it true?"

"Does it matter?"

"I guess not. But if I put my hand between your legs, like you just did to me, I'd rather not be surprised."

"If I let you put your hands between my legs, then you'll know me well enough to not be surprised."

She pushed him under the hot water then, and went to get Flynn some fresh clothes and make coffee.

"The way to march a thousand miles and win a battle
is to have the other side do all the marching."

Max Cobalt

Chapter 36

After Flynn had showered and put on clean clothes, he sat down
with Ning.

She put a fresh cup of coffee in front of him.
"Feeling better?"
"Some."
"The first thing you have to do is get rid of that head."
"The obvious solution would be to give it to the police. They would
be able to match the head to the girl, and connect the girl to Johnny
Tran. Of course, that is still a long way from a conviction, nor does it
solve the immediate problem."
"What's the immediate problem?"
"The immediate problem is that Johnny Tran, and by extension,
the Vietnamese mafia, sees me as an obstacle. They are upping their
game with each encounter. I made a mistake early on and they caught
me surveilling Tran. Since then, they have been on me like fish sauce
on rice. The next time we meet, they try to take me out in a parking
garage. That doesn't work, so they try to frame me. Now the head of the
one person who helped me shows up on my doorstep."
"Then it is time to bring the fight to them and quit staying in reac-
tive mode. Go on the offense."
"I agree."
"So bring the head to the police, point the police at Johnny Tran
and get the police to do your dirty work," Ning said
"There is, however, a huge down side with that solution. Going to

the police invites them into my business. They'll want to know why the head ended up here and how I'm involved. I can't tell them how I'm involved without exposing my connections."

"Can I ask what you're involved in, and now I'm involved in?"

"Truthfully, it's better if you don't know. That way, you can't be implicated if it all goes south."

"Okay. But is what you're involved in illegal?"

"Not technically. I was contracted by an underground source to persuade a business rival to live and let live."

"That business rival being Johnny Tran?"

"You catch on fast."

Ning was silent, sipping her coffee.

"If this was Cobalt, and this was a normal, hostile, business negotiation, how would you and Cobalt handle it?" Flynn asked.

"First, Max would never let it get to this level. He would consider it an 'unstable' situation. He would either back up and go at the problem from another direction, back off entirely, or smash it into a thousand pieces."

"My kind of guy."

"Max is unpredictable. It's one of the reasons he is so successful. Just when his opponent thinks they have him boxed, they find out he was never there to begin with."

"I don't understand."

"Once we were in a very intense, very protracted business battle. All of Max's acquisitions are intense, but this one was more so. They threw everything at him they could to stop him from gaining control of the company. It was an exhausting, money draining, time wasting exercise in futility...on their end. It cost Max very little but it looked like he was spending a fortune.

"When I asked him why, he said, 'the way to march a thousand miles and win a battle is to have the other side do all the marching.'"

"That is all very Sun Tzu, but what's it supposed to mean?"

"It means Max was never fighting them. They were fighting themselves, thinking they were fighting Max."

"And this is apropos to our situation, how again?"

Ning sighed. "So far you have been fighting a predictable war. However, the two flaws I see, are one; they are on the offense and you are on the defense, and two; each move is predictable. Tit for tat. In order to take back the battle, you need to hit them where they don't expect, using tactics they haven't thought of."

"How do we do that?" Flynn asked, intrigued not so much by her analysis, but by the way her mind worked.

"Well, we start with my nail tech's head..."

"Always mystify, mislead and surprise the enemy if possible."

Stonewall Jackson

Chapter 37

The key to winning any battle is actionable intelligence and using that to create the element of surprise.

Without information, and the element of surprise, you're doomed before you start. Flynn needed both, and both were in short supply.

Flynn immediately went over his office with counter-surveillance equipment and found the bug under his chair. They had been listening in on everything. No wonder Flynn was always a step behind.

Flynn put a finger to his lips and motioned Ning over to the chair and pointed to the device.

Ning nodded her head in understanding.

Flynn knew you needed to expect the unexpected with the Vietnamese. They were clever and smart but not good under pressure. They can't think on their feet, or adapt to changing circumstances easily. They can't adjust well if their plan fails. They need to fall back and regroup. Something you cannot let them do.

Flynn knew you could level the playing field if you stood up to them with zero fear. They are basically cowards, so they need to spend a lot of time going over details before feeling comfortable to execute.

They want you to be cowering in the corner with your tail between your legs before they'll pounce, or they won't have the courage to attack you on their own. They only attack the weak, or when they are in a position of numerical superiority. If you aren't weak, or outnumbered, then they will weaken you until they can attack without fear of losing.

So Flynn added a fast paced "chaos theory" based fighting style to the plan.

Since he now knew they were listening to him, he could feed them misinformation as he played loud Rap music, on a continuous loop, something they hated. Flynn and Ning spoke in each other's ear, or wrote out anything needing clarification. Flynn let enough slip to have them running in the wrong direction.

After going over various plans and discarding them for one reason or another, they settled on a method of attack.

For gathering intelligence, Flynn explained, he usually did it the old-fashioned way. He talked to people and either sweet-talked them into giving him information, or threatened them. Using that info, he then surveilled his subjects to learn more.

"That's when everything went to shit. I had information from a credible source..Her head is now sitting in that box over there. And I picked up Johnny Tran at one of his restaurants. But he made me. He must have checked me out and got spooked. Because then he came at me immediately, which means, he fucked up as well. He should have let me think I wasn't on to him, and surveilled ME."

"So do you have any other cards up your sleeve?"

"As a matter of fact, I do. I've actually been saving it for a special occasion such as this."

Flynn walked to a closet and brought out a large box. He opened it and brought out what looked a large, four-legged, electronic spider. At the top of each leg was a propeller. On top of the central shaft, was a video camera.

"What is it?"

"It's a video helicopter drone."

At the sound of 'helicopter' Ning was instantly intrigued.

"I used to be a helicopter pilot in my other life in Thailand."

"You never told me that."

"It's how I met Max Cobalt. I flew a chopper for the Thai military."

"Good. Now you can fly a chopper for me," Flynn smiled. He tossed a remote control device over to Ning.

Ning was immediately absorbed. She had the remote control immediately dismantled.

"Got any batteries?"

"Yeah, hold on! Let me finish explaining."

"Okay, sorry. Go ahead."

"What this puppy will do is aerial surveillance. See that video camera on top? It pans, swivels and zooms. It also has parabolic audio and low light capabilities. You can activate, record, and operate the camera via the remote control."

"Anything else?"

"Yeah. I don't use this during the day because it is too noticeable. But at night, it runs nearly silently and is almost invisible."

"What are those?" Ning asked, pointing to what looked like tiny missiles slung under the four wings.

"What do they look like?"

"30.06 cartridges for a rifle."

"That is exactly what they are. Your very own air-to-ground missiles. That was my addition, but they're useless."

"How so?"

"Because there is really no aiming mechanism. The video gives you a view from up top, but not anywhere near where the missiles are aimed. So there is no way of hitting a target with any accuracy. You can sort of line it up in the general direction, and if you were aiming for the next state you might hit it."

"But will they fire?"

"Yes. I hooked up a small firing pin on a spring, activated by electronic impulse. You arm them, then push this button here. It sends a pulse to the spring and releases it. The spring pushes the firing pin into the cartridge, cartridge goes bang."

"Neat. I want to try it."

"Not so fast…"

Flynn dug some batteries out of his desk drawer and loaded them into the enclosed space.

Ning flipped the 'ON' switch and started powering the drone up. The four rotors whirled, then buzzed like angry hornets as they increased velocity. Using the two thumb controls, she lifted the drone off the table, held it steady, then lowered it back down again.

"You have to…"

"Quiet."

Ning again lifted the drone off the table, this time she sent it across the room, and into the bathroom. Flynn punched some keys on the computer, and turned the screen around to face her.

"Now flip on the video."

Ning toggled the switch, and video of the bathroom came full color onto the computer screen.

"Flying by video screen is kinda tricky. You need to…"

"Shut up, Flynn. I've got to concentrate," Ning sing-songed.

Ning flew the drone around the office, making stops in every room. She flew up and hugged the ceiling, then flew low and scraped along the floor.

"I want to take it outside. How is it in the wind?"

"Unpredictable."

"What kind of payload can it deliver?"

"What do you mean by 'payload'?"

"How many pounds can it lift?"

"Oh. Maybe five pounds maximum."

"How do I arm it?"

"Like I'm going to tell you. You're already scaring me with that thing. Besides, play time is over. We've got the head to deal with." Flynn said.

"She was your informant. I think you should do it."

"She was your nail tech. You had a closer relationship with her than I did."

"Yeah, but she slept with you," Ning retorted.

"She didn't 'sleep' with me. She slept on the couch."

"Okay then, she spent the night with you. Don't be a baby. It's just a head."

In the end, they agreed to flip a coin. Flynn lost, which meant he had to saw through the top of the head with a hacksaw and scoop out the contents of the brain pan.

Flynn hated maggots.

"The battlefield is a scene of constant chaos. The winner will be the one who controls that chaos, both his own and the enemies."

Napoleon Bonaparte

Chapter 38

The box arrived at the produce delivery door of the Dac Biet restaurant exactly on time.

The delivery driver banged loudly on the metal door with his fist until someone came to sign for the package. The package was addressed to Johnny Tran. Flynn guessed that a delivery to Johnny Tran would be opened by him personally. No one would dare open it in his absence.

The delivery door was opened by a surly chef in a bloodstained butcher's smock. He signed for the package and waved the delivery driver away. Flynn and Ning had retreated to the roof of a nearby apartment house so they could watch the package being delivered.

The wait was long and uneventful. In truth, they weren't even sure what they were waiting for, but both figured they would know it when they saw it.

The "Chaos" fighting style wasn't a fighting style at all, but based on a loose set of actions which could be employed in any number of fluid situations. It wasn't designed to kill, but more to inflict uncertainty, panic, and confusion. It was a 'Drag and Drop' style of urban-based mayhem.

Their wait came to an end when they heard a muffled explosion, followed by black smoke being vented out through the restaurant's exhaust.

Johnny Tram stopped by the Dac Biet restaurant to eat lunch as well as pick up his weekly "protection" payment. He also used the restaurant for one of his bases of operations. He kept more than one scattered around the city. Each base conformed to a specific task. He used the Dac Biet Restaurant to dispose of victim's bodies.

To that end, he added a meat cutting room to the kitchen, complete with industrial sized meat grinders as well as heavy-duty band saws for cutting up meat…or bodies.

He walked into the kitchen after picking up his payment and was told there was a package waiting for him in back.

Flynn guessed correctly; no one wanted to touch it.

Tran saw the package sitting there and froze.

Johnny Tran hadn't survived this long by being rash and impulsive. The first question which caused him caution was, why send a package here? He walked over and inspected the package. There was nothing unusual about it. Plain box, wrapped with brown paper. The address label was computer typed with the name of a local food wholesale company. His name was also computer typed.

"When was this delivered?" Johnny Tran asked an assistant in Vietnamese.

"Sometime this morning."

"Open it."

The assistant grabbed a knife and cut through the paper wrapping.

"Carefully," admonished, Tran, standing well back.

The assistant lifted the top, then reeled backwards, clutching his hand to his nose. Inside the box was the head of Tram Ngoc, now in a state of advanced decomposition. The top was rigged with clear mono filament fishing line. Taking the top off triggered a timer.

The note covering her eyes said, "I wanted to give you a 'heads' up."

Flynn had stuffed the brain cavity with black powder, ball bearings, and a bit of C-4 he had lying around from another job.

The head exploded sending shards of splintered skull, ball bearings, and cardboard all over the kitchen. The assistant was close enough to get second-degree burns, but Johnny Tram was far enough away not to get hurt. Billowing clouds of burned gun powder set off the smoke alarms and activated the automatic sprinklers. The guests inside the restaurant panicked and ran for the doors. From their vantage point, Flynn and Ning could see them streaming out of the restaurant, choking and doubling over on the sidewalk.

"Get the car and bring it around back," Johnny Tran told another worker.

Ning powered up the drone.

Instead of the 30.06 cartridges, Flynn fitted four balloons under the drone carriage weighing exactly 1.25 pounds each, to balance the drone in flight.

The drone whined and protested, the extra weight from the balloons fighting with gravity.

Ning expected this. She had tested everything prior and knew the drone could lift exactly this much, but no more.

Flynn powered up the video. Instead of mounting the tiny camera on top as it was before, Flynn secured it on the bottom, looking down. Currently all he had a shot of was the tar roof. Ning lifted the drone off the roof and sent it hovering over the alley. The video was perfect. They were behind the roof line and out of sight of anyone below. Ning armed the mechanism.

A car came screeching into the alley and stopped by the door.

Johnny Tran, his suit ruined, and looking like a thoroughly pissed off wet rat, jumped into the back seat.

"Bombs away,"

Ning hovered the drone over the car, and pushed the firing pins on all four balloons at the same time. The balloons dropped straight down. The spark created by the electric impulse was enough so that when they burst on top of the car the entire car was immediately engulfed in flames.

Flynn had filled the balloons with homemade napalm.

The driver stomped on the gas pedal and the flaming vehicle went screaming down the alley.

Napalm, being a mixture of gasoline and laundry detergent, gels and sticks. It doesn't come off. The driver, unable to see through his flaming windshield, scraped down one side of the alley, over-corrected, and slammed into a dumpster.

Police entered the alley from one end, then a fire truck from the other, effectively cutting off any escape. The car was still blazing away as both the driver and Johnny Tran exited the car.

Johnny Tran knelt down on the ground and put his hands behind his head a safe distance away from the car.

Ning giggled. "Clean up on aisle five." She motored the drone back to the roof. It was time to get out of Dodge.

The bright light of law enforcement started to shine on Johnny Tran. So much for hiding in the shadows.

Johnny Tran had some explaining to do.

"The Vietnamese see their history as an unending series of struggles of resistance to aggression, by the Chinese, the Mongols, the Japanese, the French, and now the Americans."

Noam Chomsky

Chapter 39

Johnny Tran was released from police custody within hours.

His lawyer was at police headquarters before Johnny himself was. He was only there long enough to be photographed, fingerprinted, searched, and put into an orange prison jumpsuit, but not charged with any crime.

One of the cops involved in the booking procedure was an old friend of Flynn's. For one hundred dollars, he was persuaded to put a wireless listening bug on the underside of Johnny Tran's Armani lapel. In fact, it was the same bug that Johnny Tran had Tram Ngoc put under his chair. Flynn changed the listening frequencies, and it was good to go.

There was a certain elegance to using the equipment of your enemy against him that Flynn liked.

Tran's lawyer painted him as a victim. He was an honest immigrant, a small businessman trying to create the American Dream and caught between unscrupulous criminals.

The police, of course, bought none of it.

While Johnny Tran had been on their radar, he wasn't a big enough blip for them to take notice. Bombing a restaurant and napalming a car, however, got their attention. Since they really had nothing to hold him on, and he his lawyer was doing all the talking anyway, the brass kicked him loose.

The wireless bug worked like a charm and Flynn and Ning were listening to every word as soon as he redressed into his suit.

"Mr. Tran will you sign this form stating that these are your posses-sions, and that they were all the possessions you gave to me earlier?" Asked the duty officer.

"Yes, yes, of course," Johnny Tran said, polite and deferential to authority as always.

The duty officer handed his tanto and shoulder holster rig back with a raised eyebrow, but said nothing.

He was released into the custody of his lawyer, and walked towards his lawyer's car.

"It was bullshit, John. I wouldn't worry about it," his lawyer said, "They knew they had nothing to hold you on. The important thing now is to go about your business as usual. After all, you were the victim here."

"Oh, I plan to."

Johnny's car and driver pulled up about that time.

"Thank you again. Send your bill to my office," Johnny said to his lawyer as he got into his car.

In the car, sitting in the backseat was one of Tran's lieutenants.

"What do we know?" Tran said, as soon as the car pulled away.

"Very little. We don't even know for sure who your adversary is."

"I know who it is. The question is, how did he know where I would be?"

His soldier was silent.

"Have you swept for bugs and listening devices?"

"Yes, sir. As you asked."

"Did you sweep this car?"

"Yes, we did."

Johnny Tran fell silent, thinking through his options.

Flynn and Ning smiled from four blocks away. They had no reason to follow Johnny Tran since the transmitter would telegraph his loca-tion. They just had to keep within the sending radius of the bug.

"How's Wee doing?" Flynn asked out of the blue. "He got cut pretty bad the other night."

"He's doing okay. Nothing he can't handle. Cobalt's been keeping him company. He'll be released soon. 123 pieces of buckshot they dug out of him and seventy-nine stitches. He's milking it for everything it's worth."

"Cobalt has him on light duty when he returns to work?"

"If you can call watching the Cartoon Network and "The Simpson's" 'light duty."

"How did you guys meet?"

"Long story."

"Okay. So you were going to tell me about being transgendered in Thailand...?" Flynn said, smiling.

"I was? I don't remember ever saying that."

"Don't they call that a 'Lady Boy' in the Land of Smiles?"

"No, they call it 'female' in Thailand."

"Come on! This is what partners do. They tell each other everything."

"Is that what we are now? Partners?"

"We could be."

Ning smiled, liking the back and forth banter.

"Flynn, I like you, but it would never work."

"Only because you won't give it a chance."

"I have a life, Flynn. It doesn't include you."

"You don't have a life now. You have a job, and coworkers..."

The transmitter came alive.

"Take me to my condo," Tran told the driver.

"Do you have any orders, sir?" The lieutenant asked.

"No, stand down for now. There will be plenty of time in the future to deal with Flynn." Johnny Tran said, getting out of the car. He walked up the steps and entered his townhouse. He immediately took off his ruined suit coat and threw it in the corner. The rest of his clothes followed, then he took a shower.

"I think I just wasted one hundred dollars," Flynn said.

They heard Johnny Tran as he entered his house. Next came a scratching sound as took off his suit coat. Then the transmitter became increasingly muffled as more clothes were piled on top of it. They could hear the faint sound as the shower came on in the background.

"Shit. I think we lost the bug. He's going to put on a fresh suit and we'll lose the transmitter," Flynn said, "I should have foreseen this."

"At least you now know where he lives," Ning said, "One step forward."

Flynn dropped Ning off at the hospital, so she could give Cobalt a break from keeping Wee company. They made plans to meet later at his office.

Flynn drove away, feeling good. He had upset Tran's plans, and had taken back the initiative. The trick now was to keep the pressure on, and keep Tran off balance.

Which was why Flynn didn't see the unmarked van that blew through a stoplight blocks from his office and plow right into him.

Two masked men jumped out of the van, dragged Flynn out of the crushed cab, threw a hood over his head, and pushed him into the van.

Johnny Tran had bugged Flynn's yellow cab, too.

"The highest levels of performance come to people who are centered, intuitive, creative, and reflective - people who know to see a problem as an opportunity."

Deepak Chopra

Chapter 40

Flynn was brought back to the same restaurant he had bombed earlier in the day.

He was hooded and treated none too gently. He was slammed down in a chair, his hands and feet zip-tied to the arms and legs. He was completely immobile. Once they had him secure, they left him there.

Flynn, of course, had no idea where he was. The black cowl covering his face completely blocked out any vision. Instead, he had to rely on his other senses.

Hearing: Metal noises and what sounded like banging pots and pans in another room. When they left after tying him up, there was the noise of a heavy door closing.

Smell: Asian food smells, coupled with produce, and the lingering odor of fish. There was also the strong aroma of old smoke.

Touch: The temperature was chilly. The floor felt like concrete. The chair he was sitting in felt like wood. He sensed the room was fairly large.

Flynn strained his senses some more. He heard the faint sounds of traffic on a busy street, an occasional car horn. A slightly rotted, putrid smell, of organic material gone bad. The underlying stench of bleach.

Flynn guessed he was in a walk-in refrigerator at a restaurant. Possibly even the Dac Biet restaurant.

Flynn continued the train of thought.

Weapons: None, except a small folding pocket knife, if he could get to it. He was given a cursory pat-down to find his gun. They found his backup weapon in his ankle holster as well. However, if he was in a kitchen, then knives would be lying around. In fact, a kitchen had hundreds of improvised weapons handy.

Flynn started working on the chair's arms. His captors had tied his wrists so he was able to use his body, his shoulders and upper arms, to work the chair arms back and forth. If the chair was wood, the arms were probably only held in place with a dowel.

His thoughts were interrupted when the door opened again. He felt a rush of warmer air, then his hood was loosed and yanked off, along with what felt like half his scalp. Flynn took a quick look around. He was in a meat cutting room.

Not good.

Johnny Tran was standing opposite him in a new suit.

"You pose a problem of major proportions," Tran said, eyeing Flynn.

"Yes, but would you take me seriously if I posed a problem of minor proportions?"

"Congratulations, then. I'm taking you seriously now."

"Then my job is done. I'll be leaving."

Tran smiled and walked over to an industrial sized meat grinder and turned it on. It hummed to life. Tran pushed another button and stainless steel rollers, each with half-inch long teeth started spinning, deep in the bowels of the device.

"If you think you have problems now, kill a cop, and your problems at the moment will pale in comparison."

"Ex-cop. You're a citizen now, remember?"

"You think my buddies on the force will feel that way?"

"If I kill you, there would be a body. If there is no body, then there is…nothing."

"Except hate and animosity. The police know I'm watching you. I paid someone one hundred dollars to put the bug you put under my office chair under your lapel. They'll put two and two together when I disappear. That's what they do."

"Thanks for letting me know that." Tran walked to the door, opened it briefly, and spoke to a soldier rapidly in Vietnamese.

While Johnny Tran's back was turned, Flynn studied the chair. It was a wooden chair, just as he suspected. It was sort of an old fashioned, wooden office chair, the kind with arms and thick wooden legs.

The question was, could he break the chair with his body weight alone? He answered his own question when he snapped one of the dowels holding the chair arm in place.

Johnny Tran came back.

"Tram Ngoc told me you actually grind up bodies with that machine. Here's my question; what do you do with the bones?"

"American ingenuity at work. The grinder will grind up all but the biggest bones," Johnny Tran said. "Of course, it won't grind up a thigh bone. Skulls are also problematic. So for those we use a hammer mill."

"What do you do with the ground meat?"

"Vietnamese sausage, of course. We're a wholesale distributor. We sell it all over the Midwest. Our sausage is very popular, you know. You're going to find out. I'm going to feed you piece by piece into that grinder…Alive."

With that, Tran picked up a bone-in, pork shoulder and tossed into the bin. The grinder made obscene chewing sounds, then ground pork came out the other end seconds later.

"You are a hopelessly sick fuck."

With that, Flynn stood up, taking the chair with him, then slammed his entire two hundred and twenty-five pounds down on the chair, smashing it to pieces. The arms came off in his hands and the legs of the chair dangled around his ankles. It was like Flynn had extra wooden appendages.

Tran smiled. At the sound, two more soldiers came into the room. Tran motioned them to stay where they were. Tran drew the tanto from under his arm.

"If you want to have a knife fight, give me a weapon."

Tran picked up a kitchen steel, used to sharpen chef's knives, and threw it to Flynn.

"Use that."

Flynn picked up the steel. As a weapon, it was useless. Instead of a blade, it had a round, metal tube that chef's drew their knives back and forth on to sharpen them. It had no point.

The two men started circling each other.

"It's always funny until someone gets hurt. Then it's just hilarious."

Bill Hicks

Chapter 41

Ning went into Wee's room and found Wee getting ready to be discharged from the hospital early.

"Are they sick of you already?" Ning asked Wee.

"I know I sure am," said Cobalt.

"They were able to appreciate my wit and humor here, unlike you Ning." Wee said.

The nurse rolled her eyes as she walked past Ning.

"The orderly will be here to take you down to the lobby. You have to ride in a wheelchair," the nurse said.

"Only if you sit in my lap all the down in the elevator."

"If I sit in your lap, we'll need to take you back to ICU when I scratch your eyes out," the nurse rejoined, keeping up the banter with Wee.

"I like the feisty ones."

"I'll push him down to the lobby," Cobalt said, "I'll even push him down a flight of stairs if you want."

"Hospital regulations. The orderly will be here shortly."

Wee still had a bandage wrapped around his neck and his shoulder was encased in plaster, which made putting on his clothes difficult. Ning turned around and let the men figure it out in privacy. Much swearing on both parties' behalf and ten minutes later, Wee was dressed.

"Cobalt, does your medical plan cover in-house nurses?"

"No, but it covers an in-house kick in the ass."

"Wounded in the line of duty, Cobalt. Saving my partner from the murderous clutches of a psychopathic, sword-wielding..."

"Saving me?" Ning said incredulously. "I remember it differently..."

"In Thailand I got shot in the ass and got a medal."

"In the US if you get shot in the ass, the best you'll get is an enema and canceled medical insurance. I'll be happy to arrange for an enema if you want," answered Cobalt.

Cobalt drove home and both of them settled Wee on the couch. Wee gestured to Ning to get him the remote, then pushed it even further by asking her to cook for him.

"Sorry, places to go, things to do," Ning said.

"Oh?" Wee asked, "Another date with Flynn?"

Ning reddened. "We aren't going on a date."

"Then why are you blushing? He only wants to get into your pants."

"Maybe I'll let him into my pants."

"Ha! You know I'm the only man who can put up with you. Maybe Cobalt, but he hardly counts. He pays you to be nice to him. What happens when Flynn finds out your 'secret'?"

"Speaking of that, Cobalt, you told him I was transgendered?"

"I might have let it slip. Was I not supposed to? It's not like you're shy about it, you know."

"Men are such assholes."

Cobalt and Wee looked at each other, shrugging their shoulder, as if asking 'what's the big deal'?

"Look Ning," continued Wee, "here's the question we've all been wanting to ask; Do you stand up when you pee or not?"

"Men are such assholes," Ning repeated, and left the room.

Ning went to Flynn's office expecting him to be there. She picked the lock like a pro, and let herself in when he didn't come to the door. The office was empty. No one had been there. A small inkling of dread crept into her stomach. What were some of the possible explanations?

He could be out cruising in his cab and simply forgot about their meeting.

He could have decided to have dinner without her.

Alternatively, it could be Johnny Tran was smarter than they gave him credit for.

Door number three felt right.

To make sure, she walked to the parking garage to see if Flynn's cab was in its place. What she found was a crumpled heap of yellow metal.

When the cops got to the accident scene and didn't find a driver, they ran the plate. The cop on the scene knew Flynn and rather than have the car impounded, had the tow truck driver take it back to Flynn's garage. He knew Flynn was good for it and besides, the city paid the towing charges anyway.

Ning walked back to Flynn's office.

Okay, if he was in an auto accident, then chances are he was in a hospital. She called around to the various hospitals, identifying herself as his wife and asked if he had been admitted.

Two hours later: Nope, nada, zip, zero.

She grabbed the helicopter drone, the four-30.06 cartridges, and headed out the door.

Her problem was; she didn't even know where to begin looking. The only place she could think of, and she knew it was a long shot, was back to the Dac Biet Restaurant. Surely, after the ruckus earlier Tran wouldn't take a kidnap victim back there.

She climbed back on the roof to where they were before and powered up the drone. Maybe she could use it to peek in through the kitchen windows.

There was only one set of windows, and they were set apart from the delivery entrance door. Ning hovered the drone outside the windows and flicked on the video.

At first, she could see nothing but white and realized the windows were reflecting sunlight back at the camera, washing out the picture. She adjusted the drone out of the sunlight, and realized she had another problem. Now the interior was too dark to pick up a picture. She flipped on the low-light capability, and a picture slowly focused on the computer screen.

It was two men, circling each other. Johnny Tran was armed. Flynn wasn't.

She was in time to watch Flynn's murder play out.

"No hard guy's not scared when another hard guy's knife is coming at you. You're scared, obviously, but you've to act less scared than he is."

Peter Mullan

Chapter 42

Knives are like kinky sex; what turns you on is a personal decision.

Flynn didn't like serious knife fighters. The reason was, they were more dangerous than the average bozo with a gun. With a knife, you have to get in close to do damage, that means a willingness to get hurt yourself.

Compared to a knife fighter, gun fighters are pussies. A gun fighter won't get close enough to get hurt. He can stand out of your reach and do you damage. He's a coward compared to a knife fighter. Knife fighting is up close and personal, so close you can smell your opponent's bad breath.

So close, chances are, you're going to get wet with your enemy's warm blood.

Furthermore, because a knife is a silent weapon, it has a greater capacity for ambush. You pull a gun in a crowd and everyone knows it. A real knife fighter can walk right up to you, and if you don't know the signs, can slice and dice you, and get away, before anyone even knows what happened.

Also, knives are messy. Few people, even hardened fighters, want to stand up to a knife. It takes a certain state of mind to be able to spill someone's blood the way a knife can.

A fight to the death, between professionals, is as much a mental exercise as one with weapons, or skill.

Both men knew it. There was no banter between them now, or slinging witty zingers back and forth like in the movies. Each man conserved his energy for when it mattered. Each man had his mind zeroed in on the person in front of him. They looked neither left nor right, but straight ahead into each other's eyes. They counted on seeing any movement of attack from the corner of their eyes. The shoulders of your opponent would telegraph any move.

By looking into the eyes of someone trying to kill you, it allowed you an almost eerie glimpse into their psyche. You could become one with them. It elevated you both to a plane of karmic intensity.

Johnny Tran pulled out his tanto. Flynn had no weapon, except chef's steel. As an offensive weapon, it sucked. Even so, it might do as a defensive weapon. He put the hilt of the steel in his palm with the steel running downward on his forearm in what is called the 'leopard grip'. Maybe he could use it to block Tran's thrusts instead of having his forearm sliced to shreds.

In other words, he was fucked and he knew it.

Both men moved in a circular pattern, eyes never leaving each other. Johnny Tran spun, lightning fast, and brought the tanto down. Flynn had just enough time to block, but it bit into his arm on the side.

Johnny Tran drew first blood. It gave him a psychological advantage.

Tran stepped back, and Flynn smashed forward with an elbow strike. Tran blocked it, but enough forward force went through to snap his head backward, and he spun with the blow, causing it to lose more kinetic energy.

Flynn's only advantage was his weight. Johnny Tran was faster, younger, and better armed. But Flynn outweighed him by a good seventy-five pounds.

Youth and skill can be overcome by old age and treachery.

Flynn still had the chair legs dangling from his feet as well as one arm from the chair. He pulled the chair arm into his other hand and would use it as a club if he had to.

Johnny Tran's fighting style was Asian, so he used the Samurai stance. Legs spread and slightly bowed, with the left hand out in a claw, and the right hand down with the knife.

Flynn was an ex-Ranger. He used the military stance when fighting. Legs spread, turned side-to, to present a smaller target, left arm across the body to block and the steel on the underside of the arm. In his striking hand he held the wooden chair arm.

To say that Johnny Tran was underwhelmed by the threat Flynn presented was an overstatement.

Johnny Tran's men started laying down bets on who would win.

Tran made a couple of quick slices with the tanto, more for effect than attack. Flynn blocked them easily.

Flynn knew he only had one hope. That was to hold out until Johnny Tran made a mistake. That meant he was going to get sliced and cut. He knew it. There was no way he was going to avoid it. Johnny Tran was simply too well trained, and his knife was too sharp to avoid it. Once he accepted it, Flynn put it out of his mind. Luckily, Tran didn't have his katana or this would already be over by now.

There was a faint tinkling sound in the background, but both men ignored it. The sounds of betting and wagering competed with the winding whirl of the meat grinder.

Tran lunged again. This time Flynn was ready. Flynn blocked with the steel, again sustaining a deep slice on his left arm, but nailed Tran's knife arm just behind the elbow with the chair leg. Tran spun out of reach, shaking the pain from his arm.

Flynn's arm was bleeding freely and already a puddle of blood had pooled on the floor.

Again the tinkling sound, like glass breaking.

Johnny Tran's concentration never wavered. He feinted left, but Flynn didn't fall for it. Tran retreated in order to get a more solid footing. Now, his back was to the meat grinder, which whirling madly.

At that moment, the glass window behind Flynn smashed inward, and Johnny Tran made his mistake.

He glanced away from Flynn to see what the disturbance was. That was all it took. Flynn sprang forward swinging the chair arm from the shoulder, putting all his weight behind the blow, ducked under Tran's knife arm, and caught Johnny Tran square on the side of the kneecap, instantly breaking his leg.

Flynn continued his swing, his arms scooping Tran up under the knees and pushing Tran's head into the meat grinder. Tran's samurai pony tail flopped into the hopper, and bounced over the metal teeth, but lacking weight and downward pressure, refused to catch.

Flynn seeing what was happening, decided American ingenuity needed a little help. He turned the chef's steel in his hand and forced it into Johnny Tran's mouth lengthways, using it as leverage to force Tran's head backwards. The ponytail slid between the teeth of the rollers, then got caught in the grinding wheels.

Tran's head was yanked backwards with the strain. He lifted Johnny Tran further upward. Tran started whipping his head back and forth frantically, trying to pull his ponytail out of the rollers. The teeth caught his ponytail securely, and pulled Tran's head straight into the grinder. No sound came from Johnny as the metal teeth started biting into his skull.

Johnny Tran was wrong. An industrial meat grinder will chew up a human skull.

Tran's body flopped in the grinder, and spasmed. Flynn didn't bother to watch the bloody gruel that came out the other end. Instead, he picked up Tran's tanto and got ready for the rush from his men.

With their leader getting steadily turned into ground, bloody, beef, the first man in the back rushed out the door; then the other, deciding discretion was better than being turned into hamburger, followed him.

Flynn slid down the machine, onto the floor, spent. Tran's legs were slowly moving up the side of the machine as the spinning grinder chewed up more and more of Tran's body. Flynn's arm was still draining blood and he needed to stop it or he would pass out from blood loss. He started looking around for something to staunch the blood flow. That was when his eyes went to the shattered window.

On the floor was the broken, bent drone.

"A real friend is one who walks in
when the rest of the world walks out."

Walter Winchell

Chapter 43

Ning came in through the service entrance to the restaurant, then walked through the hanging plastic strips into the outer meat cutting room. She saw a heavy door straight ahead. If Johnny Tran was still there, she was going to shoot him.

Fuck him and his Samurai, Bushido, bullshit. Let's see how well his sword is against a seventeen shot 9mm, she thought.

Instead, she found Flynn sitting on the floor in a pool of his own blood. There was half a torso and a pair of legs dangling down beside him. She went back out into the kitchen, grabbed some clean kitchen smocks and some black duct tape.

Without a word she knelt down, folded the smocks and wrapped the cloth around his arm. Then used the duct tape and wrapped the whole thing up over his elbow.

"You'll live. You and Wee will have to argue about who received the most stitches."

"That was some serious helicopter flying to be able to break through that window," Flynn said, smiling.

"Yeah, I didn't think it was going to work. I kept having visions of it bouncing off the glass."

"How'd you do it?" Flynn asked, as Ning helped him up.

"I fired those cartridges at the glass. I tried to get them close enough to weaken it, then I hoped for the best and flew the drone straight into the window."

"You mean there were 30.06 shells ricocheting around here, and no one noticed?"

Ning smiled.

"How long you think that will hold?" Flynn asked, indicating the bandage.

"Why?"

"We got one more job to do."

"Where are the girls?" Flynn said to the owner of Perfect Nails Salon.

"All girls out there doing nails!" The owner wasn't at all sure about this big American with his duct-taped arm, leaking blood. Where was Johnny Tran's 'protection' when he needed it?

Flynn read his mind.

"He's not coming. He won't be coming ever again. However, I'm going to keep on coming until you tell me what I want to know. In fact, why don't I call the police now and tell them you're running a prostitution ring out of this nail salon?"

"No, no, you no understand."

"Look familiar?" Flynn pulled out Johnny Tran's tanto blade and held it up.

The nail shop owner paled. He knew it very well. It was the same knife used to cut off his fingers a month earlier.

"Tell me where the girls are, or I'll cut off the rest of your fingers."

"He no tell me," the shop owner whined.

"I know where they are," said a woman behind them. "Leave him alone. He knows nothing."

The three got in a car and drove to the industrial section north of town.

"In there," the woman said, indicating a building on the left.

"How many guards?"

"At least two, maybe more."

Flynn flexed his fingers making sure they still worked, then took the 9mm from Ning. He checked the magazine to make sure it was loaded, then chambered a round.

"Stay here," Flynn said to Ning.

"You go, I go."

"Then stay in back of me."

Flynn checked the windows first, but couldn't see any signs of anything. No troops, no movement of any kind.

It didn't feel right. There was no electricity in the air of latent violence.

Flynn pushed Ning to one side of the door, out of the way of any bullets that might come his way, and took the door.

He rushed into the warehouse. Gun arm outstretched, safety off, pointing the gun wherever he looked. Nothing.

They carefully searched the entire warehouse. No bad guys. No girls. Only one locked door remained. Flynn used a well-placed kick to where the lock met the door jamb. The door burst open.

The stink assaulted them first. It took a while for their eyes to adjust to the dark. There were about thirty girls inside between the ages of twelve and eighteen, living off of rice and bottled water, . There were mattresses on the floor, and a bucket in the corner. Many of the girls had bruises, some had open running sores. Ning went in and motioned Flynn to stay outside.

After about ten minutes the girls filed out of the room, blinking into the sunlight.

Flynn just motioned them towards the door.

Ning came out with the last one, a small girl no older than thirteen. "Aren't you going to call Immigration?"

"What good would it do? As fucked up as Immigration is, they'd be mistaken as Mexicans and probably ship them off to Mexico."

"You're just going to let them wander off free?"

"Why not? They certainly earned their freedom. They'll find other Vietnamese, trust me. The Viet community will take them in."

When they went back to the car, the woman and girls were gone.

Lo Chin went through security at Des Moines International airport without a problem. Nor did he expect any. He was well insulated from anything on the ground level of his businesses. News travels fast in the Vietnamese community, and Lo Chin had lots of spies. He spared a quick thought for Johnny Tran as the United flight lifted off the tarmac. He was surprised Johnny had lasted as long as he did.

He didn't mourn the loss of his lieutenant. They're plenty of people in the ranks willing to take his place. The girls also could be replaced inside of a month.

In the grand scheme of things, a minor business loss, nothing more. But he committed to memory the names of those involved, all the same.

A day of reckoning would come.

"When we were talking about this, an idea for this master vigilante, it was an urban guerilla. One of my ideas was that he would be a member of the police force who turned on the government."

David Lloyd

Chapter 44

"You be like, a one man wrecking ball when it comes to my competitors, Flynn."

Lamar was sitting in Flynn's East side office. Flynn's arm had been stitched up, and he wore bandages the entire length. There had been some nerve damage, but nothing that three hours in surgery and one hundred thousand dollars in insurance money couldn't fix.

Flynn used a wooden ruler on his desk to slip down between the bandages and scratch an itch that was driving him crazy.

"It certainly seems to always work out well for you, Lamar." Flynn observed.

"Don't it, though."

"What do you attribute all that good luck to?"

"I'm thinking it's the saintly life I lead, Flynn."

"So what's next for the 21st. Century pimp? Are you going to engineer another housing bubble? Maybe a global recession?"

"I could steal one hundred times more, and live one hundred times longer, and never even approach what you whitebreads steal in a day."

"How is it Lamar, I always fall into shit, and you always come up smelling sweeter each time?"

"Are you trying to say something, Flynn?"

"I just keep thinking. You always come out ahead. With that situation with DOP, you took over his trade. Now with the Vietnamese in the wind, you'll be taking over the Asian girl trade, not to mention the nail salons. It could be you have good karma. Of course, a more suspicious person than me might think you had an inside track."

"How come you never smoked that cigar I gave you? God damn, Flynn, that's a Cuban." Lamar said, changing the subject, and indicating the cigar he had given Flynn after the botched poker game raid still sitting in the pencil caddy.

"Because I don't smoke, you know that. Another thing, how come Johnny Tran never came after you? His beef was with you, not me. Why did he come directly at me?"

"Do you know how expensive these are?" Lamar picked up the cigar, smelled it, then started snipping the end off with his pocket knife.

"Don't light that fuckin' thing up in here, Lamar."

"I wouldn't dream of it, Flynn." Instead, he used his pocket knife and wiggled the tip of the blade into the cigar and coaxed a listening device out of one end and threw it on the desk in front of Flynn.

"Maybe I'm always one step ahead of you Flynn, because I'm always ten steps ahead of you."

Flynn looked at the bug, and pushed it around on his desk with the wooden ruler.

"You're a special kind of asshole, you know that Lamar?"

"Later, gator," Lamar said, strolling out the door.

The doorbell rang.

Ning was doing something in the kitchen. Wee ignored it. Cobalt sighed, and went to answer the door.

Flynn was standing there looking ill at ease in a suit with flowers in his hand. His arm was still bandaged, and he had to cut the sleeve off his suit to get it to fit.

"Are those for me?" asked Cobalt.

"I came to formally ask your permission to take Ning out."

Cobalt looked at Flynn. He was serious. Cobalt, always a sucker for old-fashioned manners said,

"Let me see if she's in."

Cobalt walked down the hallway and into the kitchen.

"It's for you, Ning."

Ning took her apron off, wiping her hands as she went. She gave Cobalt a quizzical look.

"Don't look at me," he said, putting his hand up in mock surrender.

Ning went to the door and returned a moment later with Flynn holding the flowers Flynn had brought her. She kissed him on the cheek.

"Let me put these in some water."

"I think I'm going to puke," said Wee, watching the drama unfold.

Flynn wandered over to the couch and sat down. Since Wee's left arm had been injured, and Flynn's right arm was hurt, they both grunted and strained theatrically to make adjustments for their injured limbs.

"How many stitches did you get?" asked Wee.

"Not as many as you."

"Ha! Pussy Americans. Do you think you're going to get into Ning's panties?"

"Would you think less of me if I didn't try?"

"The Asian way is to ask the elder brother for permission first."

Both men burst out laughing.

"Here, have some wine. It dulls the pain," Wee said, pouring Flynn a glass.

"Gimme that remote," Flynn said, grabbing it out of Wee's hand. "We are *not* watching "Simpson's" reruns."

"What's the matter with "The Simpson's"? It is social satire at its best."

"If you want social satire, watch 'Shameless.'"

"Ha! Who are you calling shameless? I'm not the one going out with a Lady Boy..."

Ning and Cobalt watched them argue over the channel selection and trade insults back and forth.

They nodded to each other at the same time.

Words unspoken and understood.

Flynn finally found a home.

"And that's the thing,
Would you recognize a seldom truth
If you heard it ring?"

Leon Russell
"Hard Rain Gonna Fall"

Epilogue

"I was with your father when he died. He spoke highly of you," Flynn said to Max Cobalt.

They were sitting in the Des Moines International Airport "Sky Cafe." Flynn was digging into a plate of nachos, heaped with jalapenos, scooping the cheese up with tortilla chips. Cobalt was having a ginger ale with a slice of lemon.

"Seriously, Flynn. My father died a long time ago, right after I was born. I never knew him. You have me confused with someone else."

"Your father died four years ago. He died right in front of me. He willingly went to his death to protect the people he loved. He was a man of honor."

"How do you know he was my father?"

"Because he told me about you. He told me you lived in Des Moines, had done well for yourself, and if I was ever in a position to help you, I should."

"That's quite a mouthful for someone's last words."

"You don't know the half of it," Flynn said, shoveling some peppers onto his chip with a fork.

"And you just decided to tell me this now?"

"Yep."

"Why wait?"

"The timing was never right. How would that conversation have gone? 'By the way, Cobalt, I hear your dead father talking to me occasionally, and he wanted me to tell you hello,' something like that?"

Cobalt smiled in spite of himself.

"He 'talks' to you, Flynn. As in, present tense?"

"Yes."

"So why tell me now?" Cobalt asked again.

"Because I no longer wanted to keep it from you. I've come to re-spect you. I didn't want to feel like there were secrets between us. Fur-thermore, I feel a lot of guilt because of what happened to your father and the role I played in it."

"What was your role in it?"

"Let's just say, for the sake of brevity, I was playing on the wrong team."

"I see."

"No, I really don't think you do. He should have killed me, Cobalt. He had every right to. I set him up to be beaten to death like an ani-mal. I was going to torture him. Instead of killing me, he saved my life. Later, I made promises to him before he died. I've lived my life since then trying to live up to my debts and obligations to your father."

Both men sat in silence, Cobalt looking at Flynn, Flynn staring back at Cobalt with orange-yellow Velveeta cheese around his unshav-en mouth.

Flynn was dead serious, Cobalt had no doubt.

For the first time, Cobalt doubted Flynn's sanity. He was starting to understand why Flynn was kicked off the police force.

"Is it possible you feel such guilt in this guy's death that you're hal-lucinating the whole thing? A sort of delayed PTSD?"

"Of course it's possible. You think I haven't thought of that?"

"But you don't think so…" The statement came out as a question.

"No."

"Why not?"

"Because sometimes, somehow, he engineers events. He also guides me in making the correct choices. He's my mentor now, almost like a father, and I've learned to trust him. Like now."

"He's guiding you now?"

"Yes. He's sitting in the chair next to you…I think."

"You think?"

"Yes, I can't see him. Only hear him. But it sounds like he is sitting there."

"What is he saying?"

"At the moment, he's not saying anything."

"And he chose this moment for you to tell me that you listen to the ghost of my dead father?" Cobalt looked at Flynn with eyebrows raised.

"There's a lot more to it than that."

"I bet there is. I can't wait."

"He's my teacher now, my moral compass."

"You're telling me this ghost is real?"

"Truthfully, I don't know. I can't explain it. I know I'm not the only one who hears him, if that makes a difference. At the end of the day, he's real to me. That's the only thing that matters.

"Look, Cobalt. I know this is a lot to take in. I know that you don't believe me. But I have an errand to run right now. I'll be back in a couple of minutes, and I'll be able to explain more. Will you wait?"

"I don't see why not. Is your ghost going to go with you or stay keeping me company?"

"I don't know. Why don't you ask him?"

Flynn got up to leave.

"Flynn? You've got cheese on the side of your mouth."

Flynn wiped his mouth with a napkin, got up and walked down the arrival concourse.

Cobalt sat alone with his thoughts, sipping his ginger ale. Unbidden, the voice of Geri Hendrix came into his mind, a boy he befriended years ago during the journey to Three Pagoda Pass. He became a Buddhist Monk and stayed in Asia to help the refugees.

"Many things are a part of this world, Mr. Cobalt that you can't see, and can't know. It doesn't mean they don't exist."

Into his mind came an image of Geri Hendrix and a mysterious stranger everyone called "The Monk." The Monk spoke next.

"Why do you find it so hard to conceive that there are greater forces at work in the Universe than the ones you can see and feel? You cannot see the wind, but you can't deny that it exists, or its power in a hurricane."

It was true; he had seen things in Asia which existed, but didn't fit into his view of reality.

Cobalt looked over at the empty chair.

"Is it true you're my dead father, and you're sitting with me?" Cobalt asked the empty chair, feeling like a total idiot.

With startling clarity, a voice in his mind said,

"I am if you want me to be. The choice of your belief is yours, not mine."

Cobalt came out of his reverie to see a little girl, about four years old, standing in front of him, looking deep into his eyes. She had dark hair and big eyes.

"Look Mommy, it's Daddy. But he's younger!"

Cobalt looked up to see Flynn standing there, also looking at him. Standing beside Flynn was a woman, a little younger than he was, very tan, with shoulder length dark hair, obviously the girl's mother. She was staring at Cobalt, crying softly, tears sliding down her cheek.

"Oh Daddy, I should have known," she said.

"Max Cobalt, I'd like you to meet your step-mother, Mia Cobalt, and your sister, Mia Lynn," Flynn said, introducing everyone all around.

The little girl, without a second hesitation, jumped into Max Cobalt's lap and started stroking his face tenderly.

"I missed you forever," Mia Lynn said.

And Flynn's ghost approved.

The End.

I see you've made it to the end of this book. I'm glad you liked it enough of it to get all the way through.

If you liked the book, would you be open to leaving me a 4 or 5 star review?

You see, I'm a self-published author. I don't have big ad budgets, editors, or a publishing house behind me or helping me.

All I have is a few friends and readers like you.

When readers are able to give me positive reviews, it helps me out in a big way. In addition it is my readers which tell me what I did right, and what I did wrong. They tell me if I should continue a series, if they liked (or hated) the characters, etc.

Readers like you are the only thing I have, and the only thing, truthfully, I need.

You can leave a review for me at the website where you bought the book. Or you can leave a review for me on my Amazon page here: **Review Bad Karma Here**

You can also contact me here: http://JohnRebell.com and you'll receive a personal reply.

It would really mean a lot to me.

All the best to you and your family,

John Rebell

Other Books by John Rebell

The Adventure Starts Here.

Max Cobalt gets sucked into doing an overseas job. Every one but him knows it's a suicide mission.

The race is on in this action adventure to bring healthy food, and medicine to the people who need it the most.

Max, Ning, and Wee only need to stop a homicidal warlord, corrupt government officials, Big Pharm, human trafficking, child slavery, and black market organ harvesting dead in their tracks.

He's out-gunned, out maneuvered, out of time, out of luck, and on his own, against insurmountable odds.

Buy it here $3.99

Meet Flynn and James Cobalt in Mia's Journey

Mia has been abused her entire life. It started with her father and continued when she was given to her husband as payment for legal fees. Her husband, Jeffery Prescott, was a well connected lawyer who took great pleasure in using his submissive wife anyway his twisted mind desired.

Ten years later, Mia meets someone she nicknames "Daddy," for the father she never had. However, Daddy isn't who he appears to be. Daddy knows he is no action hero. He can't compete with younger, stronger, better armed men. He has to rely on his smarts instead.

A sexual sadist, a corrupt cop, a powerful family, against two unprepared, unlikely, heroes.

Buy it here $3.99

About The Author

John Rebell and his son Lennon
in Saigon, Vietnam. Circa 2006

John Rebell is an American ex pat splitting time between Southeast Asia and the Midwest USA.

Merchant seaman, private investigator, biofuel consultant, writer, and teacher. He has written over 8 non-fiction books. His non-fiction books have been critically acclaimed and one a global bestseller.

He has been married for 19 years and has one son.

His other fiction works include "Three Pagoda Pass" and "Mia's Journey"

You can contact him at http://johnrebell.com

www.ingramcontent.com/pod-product-compliance
Lightning Source LLC
Chambersburg PA
CBHW070551180626
46817CB00005B/1784